I0823701

MURDER IN THE BAPTISTRY

ALSO BY RICK NICHOLS

The John Logan Thrillers

The Judas Man

Survivor's Affair

The Affairs of Men

The Sheltering Tree

Into the Magic Night

Cold Dish

Hindsight

A 'FROM THE PULPIT' MYSTERY

MURDER IN THE BAPTISTRY

RICK NICHOLS

Keylight Books
an imprint of Turner Publishing Company
Nashville, Tennessee
www.turnerpublishing.com

Murder in the Baptistry

Cover design by Kent Holloway
Book design by William Ruoto

Library of Congress Cataloging-in-Publication Data
Names: Nichols, Rick, 1964- author.
Title: Murder in the baptistry : a novella / by Rick Nichols.
Description: Nashville, Tennessee : Turner Publishing Company, 2025. | Series: From the pulpit mysteries

Identifiers: LCCN 2024025248 (print) | LCCN 2024025249 (ebook) | ISBN 9781684428069 (paperback) | ISBN 9781684428458 (hardcover) | ISBN 9781684428465 (epub)
Subjects: LCGFT: Detective and mystery fiction. | Novellas.
Classification: LCC PS3614.I3528 M87 2025 (print) | LCC PS3614.I3528 (ebook) | DDC 813/.6—dc23/eng/20240612
LC record available at https://lccn.loc.gov/2024025248
LC ebook record available at https://lccn.loc.gov/2024025249

Printed in the United States of America

For Lisa, for letting me do this

And thanks to:

David Elder for the proofing and encouragement.

Kent for his advice.

And Ashlyn for her editorial work.

SHE SQUINTED IN THE SEMIDARKNESS. THERE was no light except for the small LED that always lit the cross on the wall overlooking the rows of pews. It was lit even when the church was closed.

"Can't we talk about this?"

"No," she said. "How could you do that to me?"

"Look, that was a long time ago and things have changed."

"For you, maybe," she said. "The last ten years sure changed for me. And why are we up here, anyway? It's creepy."

"I'm begging you, don't do this."

"You thought you could hide from me. Soon everyone will know your secret. What you did."

"Please don't...." The words were choked. "We were friends."

"We were," she said. "Until you betrayed our friendship. You never even wrote me, visited me. Not once."

"I couldn't. Because of...things. Please don't do this."

"Sorry. You made this bed." She turned away, heading back to the stairs. She heard a rustle of cloth, and she had begun to turn when something went over her head and around her throat. Instinctively, she grabbed for it, trying to pull it away; but it only got tighter. Her arms flailed back, trying to reach her assailant. She got one blow in on her assailant's head, she thought, but she felt a hard knee in the small of her back, arcing her torso, taking away leverage. She tried to suck air that wouldn't come. Darkness seeped into the edges of her vision, darker than the holy ground where they were. Her lungs burned and she tried to scream, but only a strangled gasp came out. The blackness creeped onward until she had no more fight left in her. Her last fleeting image was the cross before the darkness took over.

THE SMALL WOMAN SLIPPED INTO THE SHADows moving across the parking lot. Her eyes darted left and right as though she was convinced someone would be watching her, knowing what she had done. There were always gossips, and they loved a juicy tale, and she'd seen the whispers and giggles from the old bats as they huddled around.

The church lay in shadow except for the lights on the sign by the main entrance. Another lit the cross atop the steeple, but it had little effect on the parking lot below.

Then she heard the voices.

Inside the church, muffled and unintelligible because of the thick brick walls, she couldn't make out words. But there was an argument. She knew arguing when she heard it, a skill acquired in her childhood.

She increased the speed of her steps. She didn't want to be found here. She'd almost made it, when headlights hit her and the police car pulled alongside.

CHAPTER ONE

HOME

"WELL?" ELLEN ASKED HER HUSBAND.

Reverend Asa Carter looked at the quiet elm-lined street and adjusted the round rim glasses on his thin face. The houses were all older two-story homes with flowerbeds and covered porches and storage sheds. Lawns of oak and maple trees bordered the quiet street. It was tranquil, a scene from a Rockwell painting. And though Chicago had had its share of quiet neighborhoods, there was something here that Asa could not pinpoint. He found himself wondering again if he had made the right decision. It wasn't that he doubted his calling; if God had indeed called him here, then he was fine. But there was a slight nagging in his mind suggesting that maybe he was wrong. He usually had that feeling whenever a change in his life happened, so he paid it little mind. But it was still there, and sometimes he found it annoying.

"It's not Chicago," he said.

Ellen chuckled. "No, it's much quieter and slower-paced here."

"I can see that." Asa hoisted a marked box full of kitchen utensils through the door and disappeared inside. The movers had left only a few boxes that Ellen wanted to unpack herself; everything else was pretty much in place.

Ellen looked around the house and then outside. She remembered this neighborhood from her youth. She'd ridden bikes with her best friend Suzie on this street countless times, growing up. Things hadn't changed much.

When the church had called and offered Asa the pastorate position, she knew he'd been hesitant to move her back to her hometown, for a couple of reasons. Glen Pines held many memories for her, not all of them good, but the pace of city life had worn them both down. And as urban schools became more and more like fortresses, Ellen's desire to teach in a quieter place was also evident.

You couldn't get much quieter than Glen Pines. Situated in a valley between rolling forested hills, it was always said that time had slowed—or even stopped—here. As a young girl, Ellen couldn't wait to get out and head for the bright lights. Chicago had been good to her, and she had met Asa on a blind date. He'd been a detective then; meeting her had caused him to rethink his life, and he had started going to church with her and getting involved.

The second reason was her husband's love of Chicago, but it was that same city that had taken so much out of him. The pace of police work had worn him down, the burden lying heavily on his shoulders, and the only time he seemed to lay that load aside was when he volunteered at their church.

She walked into the kitchen to find him whistling as he put away some utensils in a drawer.

"Are you having second thoughts?"

Asa shrugged. "I'm sorry. I made it seem like I didn't like it here. I will be fine. It's where I'm supposed to be. With you."

She smiled. "You were here last month for the interview and preached a sermon. You can't say you didn't know. Besides, the church needs you," she said. "It needs your wisdom and your strength."

"They've been through a lot," Asa agreed. "It will take some time. For both of us." He finished, the box empty, and turned it upside down with a flourish. "What about you?"

"It definitely is kind of weird, being back here after all these years," she admitted. "I once said I would never come back."

"Yet here you are," Asa said.

She walked to him, put her arm around his waist. "Yet here I am."

"How does it feel?"

"It feels..." she paused with that reflective expression Asa knew so well: "...okay."

"Can't ask for more than that," he said. "Have you heard from Katy?"

"Yes. She texted to make sure we were settling in. She had classes and a lab this afternoon."

"Perils of med school," Asa said. He pictured their daughter in her white coat when the school had held the ceremony for the new class. Katy was in Ohio, studying to be a pediatrician. He looked around. "Anything else left?"

"Just some pictures. Not sure where I want them."

"I'll hang them for you when you decide."

"You have your first day of work tomorrow," she said.

He nodded, his way of telling her that he knew. "And I have a sermon due Sunday."

"Are you okay? With this?"

"I'm fine," he said and kissed her forehead.

"At least no one is shooting at you," she said.

"And no dead bodies," Asa retorted. It was an old joke still told between them. They laughed, and Asa went out to get the last box from the porch.

CHAPTER TWO

THE NEW GUY

GRACE GOSPEL CHURCH SAT ON FIVE ACRES of carefully tended landscaping, which included parking spaces and several oak trees that the city claimed were over a hundred years old and thus of historic significance. This had prevented their being cut down, and those who'd been there at the start of the building project could recall the frantic consultations with the architect and contractor over the necessary changes and the resulting blows to the budget.

The church consisted of a worship center shaped like a crude pentagon. A long two-story rectangular structure holding classrooms and the children's center jutted out from the worship center. A separate smaller building connected by a covered portico held the church administration and pastors' offices. In the back was a large storage and maintenance building with a small efficiency apartment on top.

The senior pastor's office was the largest in the admin building, located down a small hallway near the back, away from the noise of the front reception area. Behind a desk that was part of the original furniture sat Mae, the pastoral secretary. She and her husband Bob had helped found the church; they'd joined the small group of people who came together and met in a storefront for two years until the money was right and the Lord's timing was as well. Bob had gone to heaven five years ago, and Mae, despite her age, had given no thought to retirement. The church had been a source of duty for her over the decades, and even Bob's death had not erased it.

Mae turned to see Jackie, the receptionist, typing rapidly on a computer. Probably working on the order of service for Sunday. Jackie was a pleasant soul, and Mae remembered her as a young girl in the burgeoning youth department not quite two decades ago. Jackie's child would soon be joining in the activities of the youth as well. Time, Mae realized, marched on.

She rose and walked down the hallway. The pastoral door was open and she peered inside.

Asa stood with his back to the door, placing books onto the built-in bookshelves behind the large oak desk. Several empty boxes were stacked neatly beside the couch. He'd made quick work of unpacking, she thought.

"Reverend Carter?"

Asa turned. He was a tall man, slender, with round wire-rim glasses and a receding hairline. His nose was sharp, his jawline angular. He looked at Mae with eyes that exuded intelligence and kindness, but Mae figured he could give a penetrating look if so inclined.

"You can call me Asa," he answered. "No need to be so formal."

"I remember your wife," she said. "Used to come here during Vacation Bible School."

"She said it was one of the rare days when she got to eat."

"I know. I always tried to give her extra."

"That was nice of you."

"I don't suppose you ever met her mother."

"No."

"Very nice lady," Mae said and paused. "Until she wasn't. Anyhoo, do you need anything?"

"Is there a coffee machine?"

"You have a favorite cup to drink out of?"

He handed her a large cup with WORLD'S GREATEST PASTOR on it. Mae glanced at it and went out.

"Black!" Asa called out to her. "Please!"

She returned a moment later. "Are you settled in?"

"Yes, I think so," Asa answered. He accepted the cup with a nod. "Anything I need to know about?"

"Did you get your building keys?"

"Yes, if I can keep them straight."

She didn't respond. "Jackie is typing up the order of service, and Kyle wants to see you."

"Kyle..." Asa said thoughtfully. "Kyle?"

She regarded him with a stare. "Your assistant pastor."

"Ah, yes, of course," Asa said. He chided himself for forgetting the only other minister's name.

"And part-time youth pastor. We run a small ship here," Mae said. "When can he come by?"

"Any time," Asa answered.

"He's on a hospital visit. He'll drop by when he's done, I'm sure." She paused for a moment. "We're glad you are here." She turned and left, leaving Asa to stare after her.

Six months ago, the pastor of the church had run off with a member's wife. He'd also managed to abscond with several thousand dollars of church money. The scandal had understandably shocked and stunned the church, which had struggled along with several pastors filling in until Asa had been hired. It was a tough thing to be betrayed by someone who had been so loved and well-thought-of. It was not the first time a church had experienced such things and would not be the last, Asa knew. He had to build trust and provide leadership, vision, and stability for these people. It would happen, but maybe not overnight. Incidents like that could fracture a church, even split a faction off into seceding. That, he wanted to prevent. But he was coming in as new as a baby, and congregational groupings and cliques here were not yet clear to him. They tended to follow certain patterns, and Asa was sure he'd find out soon enough. He'd felt God calling him to come here. To help the church, certainly, he felt; but was there something more? Asa couldn't say.

He finished arranging his desk the way he wanted, including a picture of Ellen and his daughter. And Ellen...well, she was already working, teaching math at the local high school. Teachers were hard to find in these parts, and they'd welcomed her with open arms. His beautiful Ellen, who had taken a broken, lost man, and helped him find his way again. *So many years ago*, Asa thought. He would not be here without her by his side.

Nearly two decades, he recalled. Two decades and three churches. This would be the biggest test of them all, so far. The bigger the church, the larger the congregation, the bigger the headaches. More buildings meant more upkeep, which meant more money needed in the church coffers, and more people always meant more ministries, more committees, more demands. Asa was aware of the burnout statistics among clergy. Many had even walked away completely from the faith. It was a sobering stat that Asa had always kept in mind. It was never easy, balancing God's work with family and yourself. This place would be no different.

He shook himself from his momentary reflection and went back to work. A large man in jeans and a polo shirt with the church logo on the breast stuck his head in. "Hello."

"Hi, Walter," Asa said. The first thing one noticed about Walter was his size. At six-foot-five, not yet thirty, Walter's huge frame filled the doorway. Blond hair in a crew cut, clean-shaven, Walter Pence's good nature countered his intimidating size.

The church custodian beamed. "Was the office cleaned good?"

"It was," Asa said. "Thank you. And thanks for hanging up my stuff."

"Oh," Walter grinned. "Did I do it right?"

"You did. Thank you."

"Anything else you need from me?"

"Nope. Probably better ask Mae. I'm kind of new yet."

Walter Pence grinned. "Okay, Pastor. Or should I call you Doctor?"

"'Asa' is fine."

"Momma never liked me calling a pastor by their first name. It was disrespectful, she said."

"Okay, then. 'Pastor Asa' is fine."

"Are you really a doctor too?"

"Not a medical one," Asa said. "I have a Ph.D. in Theology." He gestured to the diploma on the wall. "See?"

"Wow, how do you get that?"

"A lot of study and hard work."

Walter seemed satisfied. "Okay, Pastor. I'm going to check with Mae. See you later."

He was gone as rapidly as he'd appeared. Walter lived on the premises in the apartment over the maintenance building, Asa had been told. Walter's mother had died when he was about twenty, but they were members here and the women had taken him under their wing. The apartment had been built and he'd been given the job as a custodian. Several of the congregation had worked to improve Walter's reading skills, and Asa wondered if Ellen could work with his math skills. He made a mental note to ask her and returned to the business of the desk. He wanted to be ready to dive in by lunch.

CHAPTER THREE

THE TOUR

"PASTOR?"

Kyle Davis stuck his head in the doorway. Asa knew little about him, except that he had been hired a month before Asa. Fresh out of the local seminary, he'd done some work leading services at churches around the area while he attended, and the growing number of youths here had led him to wear that hat as well. He was of medium height with black hair that fell over one eye, which he was constantly brushing away as one might try to shoo a fly. He brimmed with the energy of youth and newness to the ministry, blissfully ignorant of the pitfalls that lay ahead. Asa envied him.

"You settling in?"

"Doing fine, Kyle, thanks."

"Music is ready for Sunday," he said. "Put in a couple that you said you liked."

"I appreciate that."

Kyle fidgeted a little.

"Everything okay?"

He took two steps and leaned over the desk, his face close to Asa's. His eyes shone with excitement. "Is it true?"

"What?"

"That you used to be...you know..."

Asa sighed. "A cop?"

"I heard a homicide detective," Kyle said. He sat down in one of the visitor's chairs.

"Yes, but that was before you were born," Asa said.

"Still, that must have been exciting work," the young minister went on. "Catching the bad guys, high-speed chases, shoot-outs—"

"Only in the movies," Asa said. "No chases, no shoot-outs. The only time I ever fired my service weapon was at the range every six months."

"Oh, come on, you can level with me," Kyle said.

"I am. When I was called, the crime was over. There's the dead body, and the bad guys are nowhere to be seen."

Kyle looked crestfallen. "No shoot-outs?"

"Most homicide detectives have to remember to get their weapon out of the desk drawer when called to a scene," Asa said, almost guilty of crushing the young man's idealism. "I left the shoot-outs to the SWAT teams."

"But I thought..."

"Police work is mostly paperwork," Asa explained. "You go out to the scene, there's paperwork. Every phone call to witnesses, every interrogation, everything you do on the case is logged and documented. And most of the time, a case is solved because of something the killer did or said to someone."

"Wow," Kyle's voice was almost a whisper. "I didn't know."

"Too much TV," Asa said. "Sorry."

The young man's shoulders slumped. Asa decided a change of subject was in order.

"Mae said you were on a hospital visit."

Kyle said he had been. An elderly member had gone in for surgery and was improving. "Let me take you on a tour of the church," he said.

"Well, I've kinda already—"

"Come on. I'll show you around. You couldn't have seen everything while you were interviewing."

Asa finished the coffee. He'd had worse, but not in a while. "All right."

Kyle went down the hall. "Mae, I'm taking the pastor for a tour of the place."

Mae regarded the young man with a long stare. She gave a slight sniff, then went back to her work.

The two men went out under the portico. "I don't think she likes me much," Kyle said.

"Who?"

"Mae."

"Why do you say that?"

"She seems so...aloof."

"She's been here a long time," Asa said. "Set in her ways. Remember, Kyle, this church has been under a big strain for months. People can get wary, frightened, even lose their faith. We must point them toward the truth. Toward the light. I think in time she'll warm to both of us."

"I hope you're right. By the way, there's the maintenance shed. All the tools, lawn mowers and stuff are there. Above that is the small place where Walter lives."

"I heard his mother was a member here."

Kyle nodded. "Yeah. I don't know much, other than that she

died and the church kinda adopted him. Gave him a job. The women bake and cook for him a lot, so he has a new family, you could say. He's a good guy, just challenged a little."

"What about you? Tell me about you," Asa said.

"Born and raised here, went to seminary, was finishing up and got the call from one of the deacons who knew me way back when. Asked if I could come. What can I say? A nice position right out of school."

"Certainly," Asa agreed.

"But I—well, *they*—felt I wasn't ready to be senior pastor. They were probably right."

"You will be some day, although there is always a need for music pastors, remember."

"Mae said your wife was born here?"

"Yes. Left at seventeen for the bright lights and never dreamed she'd be back."

"He had other plans," Kyle said.

"He usually does," Asa agreed.

"You living in the parsonage?"

"Yes, it's quite nice."

"Sad, really. Mrs. Kilburn having to move out, facing all the gossip, her husband doing such things."

"Where did she go?"

"To her sister in Rhode Island, I hear," Kyle answered. "Mae might know."

"Mae seems like she knows everything that happens here at the church."

"From what I've seen, she does," Kyle said.

Kyle showed him the small youth center with a few table games and chairs and a sofa. A small stage was at the far end. There were classrooms for Bible-study groups. Kyle mentioned that he had some ideas for sprucing up the place.

That led to a quick tour of the long section with more classrooms for the adults and, finally, to the worship center. In the back was a large room used for conferences and fellowship dinners and meetings. Twice, Asa tried to explain that he'd seen a lot of it when he met with the church for the interview, but Kyle seemed unfazed.

"And here is the sanctuary where all the fun is," he said.

"I know. I preached here a month ago," Asa said. It was normal to have a new hire try out the pulpit to test his preaching skills. Or to see if he could put together a coherent thought. Or if he could keep the commandments straight. Whatever the reason, it was always a good idea to give the prospective hire a test run.

"Why'd you stop being a cop?" Kyle asked.

"I was a different person then," Asa answered. "Then I met my wife and—well, things changed."

They were in the back of the sanctuary, behind the wall of the choir loft where the choir rehearsed every week.

Asa turned the question back to the young man. "Why did you go into the ministry?"

"I'd wanted to be a music minister since I was eight," Kyle said. "Seeing the one at my church lead the singing, directing the choir. There was no other calling for me." He paused. "Say, you baptize people, don't you?"

"A few," Asa said.

"Let's see the baptistry," Kyle suggested. "It's nice."

"I'm sure it is. Actually, I was wanting to—"

But Kyle had already pushed the button on the elevator, and Asa sighed and dutifully followed.

"One of the deacons is in charge of assisting us," Kyle said. "They help out a lot. Nothing to it."

"Good to know."

The door opened. In front of the baptistry area were the bathrooms that served as changing rooms for the baptismal candidates. A small flowered sofa let them sit until it was time.

To the left, a drawn curtain hid what Asa guessed was the baptistry itself. Three feet of water in a pool where you stood with the candidate.

"That's pretty much it," Kyle said. "Of course, here's the pool—" He drew the curtain back, and both men started. Kyle gasped and took a step backward. "Oh, dear God..."

A body floated face down in the bluish chlorinated water. She wore cutoff shorts and a blue tank top that showed off heavily tattooed arms. Her hair was dyed bright green. Open-toed sandals hung on her feet.

For a moment, Asa was back in Chicago, under the strobe of police lights; and then he found himself pulling the body from the water, laying her face up on the tile. "Kyle, call 911."

The young man just stared for a moment.

"Kyle!"

"Nine-one-one. Right." He swallowed hard and fumbled for his phone.

What a way to begin my first day, Asa thought.

CHAPTER FOUR

INSTINCTS

Chief Ned Daniels gripped Asa's hand with his own large one and shook it with a gentleness that belied his size. Daniels was a big man with a belly that spoke of a bad diet and not enough exercise. Probably played linebacker in high school, Asa guessed.

"Finally nice to meet you, Reverend. Wish it were under better circumstances."

"Likewise, Chief," Asa said.

"I went to school with your wife, back in the day."

"Really?"

"Yeah. Quite a beauty she was."

"Uh, Chief." Asa nodded at the dead girl. "The body?"

"Oh, yeah, right." Daniels ran a hand over his face and eyed the girl lying supine on the tile.

"Heck of a way to start off your tenure here, Reverend, wouldn't you say?" Daniels said. Several other police officers scurried about.

"No ID, fifty dollars in cash...slightly damp, of course," Asa said. He knelt beside the dead girl.

"I've seen her," Daniels said. "She works at the diner. Hasn't been there long."

"She from here?"

Daniels shook his head. "Don't think so. New in town. I think Carla talked to her a couple of times."

"Carla?"

"One of my officers." Daniels motioned to an attractive female officer to come over. Carla Reed had dark eyes and hair, and, beneath the bulk of the Kevlar vest, Asa could tell she had a lithe, athletic build. "Carla, you know her?"

Reed nodded slowly. "Tara Brooks. She worked at the diner."

"What do you know about her?"

"Drifter, I think, but from Kentucky. She came into town and applied for a job at the diner. I think she was staying at the motel for now."

"How'd you come to know her?"

"Like I said, Chief, she applied for a job. Marty wanted her checked out. She did prison but had served her time, and Marty felt sorry for her and gave her a job. She thought I was trying to hassle her."

"Prison, huh?"

Reed nodded. "Yeah. But she served her time."

"Wonder what she was doing here."

"Maybe trying to start over," Asa said.

"Thanks," Daniels said to Reed. "We'll chat more later." He looked at the water and scratched his head. "How could you drown in a baptismal pool?"

"She didn't drown, Chief," Asa said.

"Huh?"

Asa pointed to her neck while Kyle watched wide-eyed. "See that indentation? Made by a ligature of some kind." He knelt further over her, looked at the eyes. "Petechial hemorrhaging in the eyes, too."

"What?"

"Signs of strangulation, Chief," Asa said.

"Uh...right, of course," Daniels said.

"Someone murdered this girl," Asa continued. "I take it the M.E. is on the way?"

"Yeah, should be here any time." Daniels turned to one of the officers. "Make sure Doc gets up here." The cop nodded and hurried to the stairs.

"Look here," Asa said. He pointed to a faint white line at her wrist.

"What's that?"

"Tan line. Maybe from a bracelet, but I haven't seen one."

"Maybe she wasn't wearing it."

Asa nodded. "Or maybe it got ripped off in the struggle. No way to know yet. But any girl that wears a bracelet long enough to get a tan line from it usually wears it, I would think."

"We'll look for it," Daniels said.

"This is like *CSI*," Kyle said. "Want me to look for clues?"

"What are you looking for?" Asa asked.

"I don't know. Exactly."

Asa nodded. "Just sit tight."

Daniels was looking around as though he knew what he was looking for. "She must have been here all night."

"I doubt that. Doc can be more precise; but, judging by the lividity and rigor, she hasn't been dead long. Six hours, maybe. The water might have affected it."

"How do you know?"

"Someone killed her. In a church," Asa said. *My church!* He rose and left the scene. There was little more he could do.

Another officer stuck his head in. "Chief, come look at this."

Asa and Kyle followed Daniels down the stairs to a single door that led outside. The officer held the door open until they were out, then pointed at the lock. There were scratch marks.

"Killer picked the lock," Daniels said.

"Make sure they weren't on there before, but that's a good assumption for now," Asa said. He walked out and across the parking lot toward the church office. Kyle caught up with him. "Anything I can do to help?"

"Yes, let's get out of here," Asa said. "The fewer people at a crime scene, the better."

Kyle looked crestfallen.

"Does she look familiar to you?"

"I've seen her at the diner. Always nice to me."

"I mean here at church."

"Oh, right. I think she was here last Sunday. Sat in the back near the door. Can't be positive, but I think I saw her. Noticed the hair, anyway."

"Did you talk to her?"

He shook his head. "Sorry, I have to admit I didn't. I think she left as soon as the sermon was over." His face suddenly brightened. "You did great up there, with all the detective stuff."

"I'm not a cop anymore," Asa said, and then wondered why he had said it. Was he trying to convince the young minister? He paused. He walked into the reception area under Mae's intense gaze, then down the hall to his office, where he plopped into his chair. Kyle sat on the sofa.

"Are you okay?"

"Just needed some air," Asa said.

"Figured you'd be used to seeing a dead body, Pastor."

"Once upon a time, yes."

Mae stuck her head in. "You all right?"

"We're fine, Mae," Asa said. "What a way to start my tenure."

"What happened?"

Asa briefly recounted the events.

Mae, to his surprise, seemed unfazed by it. "Such a tragedy. And right on top of the other stuff."

Asa agreed. "Mae, how many people have keys to the building?"

"Six or seven. Me, Jackie, you and Kyle, Walter, of course. And Doc Adams, the Deacon Chairman, and Bill the maintenance guy." She thought. "Seven."

"Okay. Daniels will probably need to talk to everyone with a key."

"But didn't the killer pick the lock?"

"Possibly," Asa said. "But you check every angle first."

"Right," Mae said. "What shall we tell the congregation?"

"You let me worry about that."

"You want another cup?" She gestured to the coffee cup and made a wry smile. "This is a better batch."

Asa nodded and smiled. "Sure. Thanks."

Kyle spoke from his place on the sofa. "So, where do we start?"

"What do you mean?"

Kyle looked at him as though Asa had three heads. "To start solving the murder!"

"First off, there is no solving. It's a police matter, and I'm sure Chief Daniels doesn't want civilians snooping around."

"Hmph," Mae snorted as she returned with the coffee. "Forgive me, Pastor. Daniels is a nice, honest man, but he couldn't find his butt with both hands, if you'll pardon the analogy."

"Really? How did he become chief?"

"Appointed by the mayor. Ned's a decent cop, but there's not been a murder here in years. He simply doesn't have the experience that..." She looked down.

"That I have?"

"I didn't say that...exactly. I also told Doc Adams to come here and fill you in as well, on what he finds on the girl."

"Doc Adams? You mean like in *Gunsmoke*?"

Mae shot him a look. "Nathan Adams is a fine doctor and the closest thing we have to a medical examiner. He's also chair of your Deacon Board and was partially responsible for bringing you here."

"I know, Mae, I was being smart."

She sniffed and left but returned a moment later. "Doc is here. You might go up and see what he says."

"Mae..."

"Remember?"

Asa nodded. "Can't find his butt with both hands."

"Good. Now shoo."

Asa looked over at Kyle. "Might as well tag along, Robin."

CHAPTER FIVE

A SECRET REVEALED

DR. NATHAN ADAMS WAS, AS FAR AS ASA HAD heard, a well-respected physician in the town. As chairman of the church deacons, Adams also had had the duty of interviewing him along with the board. Deacons were, by scripture, servants of the church and, by extension, of God. They assisted the pastor and oversaw ministries that the church ran. Deacon boards had the power to remove a pastor for cause as well as to hire them. They could be a valuable asset to a pastor—or a nagging pain in the neck.

Asa found Adams kneeling over the dead girl. Daniels stood gazing down, and Asa saw something peculiar pass through the chief's eyes. Kyle was nearly exploding with excitement, and Asa put a calming hand on the young man's arm.

"Five, maybe six hours, Ned," Adams said. "Definitely strangled."

Daniels nodded as he spoke. "Yeah, I noticed the pat-pat-patty-whatchacallits in her eyes."

For the first time, Adams saw Asa. "Sorry, Pastor. Not the way we'd like your first week to go."

"Any chance the water affected the body temperature, Doc?"

"Maybe. The heat wasn't on, so the water was pretty much room temperature. You didn't turn it off, did you?"

"It wasn't on," Asa said.

"It wouldn't be turned on until Saturday night for a Sunday morning dunk—I mean baptism," Kyle said. He noticed Asa eyeing him and gave an apologetic look.

Doc continued his examination. "Looks like some scarring on arms. This lady did some drugs years ago."

"Not recently?" Daniels asked.

"Scars are old, nothing fresh," the doc answered. He snapped off his gloves. "All I can do from here. Get her on the table, maybe I can dig up more."

"Thanks, Doc," Daniels said.

Asa turned and took the elevator back down. He found a pew and sat, staring up at the cross mounted above the choir loft.

Several minutes later, the paramedics wheeled the young lady out and Daniels came down and sat beside him.

"For what it's worth, Pastor, I'm sorry."

"Thanks, Chief."

"Where are you from?"

"Chicago."

Daniels paused for a moment. "How'd you know?"

"Know what?"

"About her time of death, the marks, the eyes. How does a preacher know that?"

"Would you believe me if I said I read a lot of murder mysteries?"

"No, although it may be blasphemous to suggest that a man

of the cloth would lie to me," Daniels retorted. "But the last one ran off and committed grand larceny, so forgive me if I am a little skeptical."

"A good trait to have in a detective," Asa said, instantly regretting the remark.

"And how would you know that?"

He sighed. "Before I turned to the ministry, I was a cop. Homicide. Chicago PD. Fifteen years."

"Seriously?"

"Yes," Asa said. "But that was a long time ago."

Daniels leaned back, and a smile crossed his face. "Well, dip me in gravy. A guy becomes a cop, then a preacher. That's something, I'd say." The smile faded. "Of course, I have to think that you come into town, new pastor and all, and we have our first homicide in years. I'm sure that's coincidence."

"It is."

"Now I have to find out who killed her."

"I didn't kill her, Chief. And if I had, I wouldn't dump the body here, in my church."

"Unless," Daniels held up a finger, "you knew that, and did it purposely to throw me off."

Asa sighed. "There's another thing. Doc said the girl was killed six hours ago, right?"

"Uh-huh."

"Middle of the night, church was locked. I didn't get my keys until eight-thirty this morning."

"But the lock was picked. You could have done that."

"So could anyone else who knows how."

"Who all has keys?"

"Mae can tell you. I've already told her to give you that information."

Daniels leaned back in the pew and glanced up at the cross. From here, you couldn't quite see the baptistry waters. "I've never done this before."

"What's that?"

"Investigate a murder."

"What about your department?"

"Nope," Daniels said. "Any advice?"

"Ninety-five percent of the information you collect will be useless, but you won't know that until you sift through it. Keep good notes. Where you go, times, places, who you talked to with contact information, and what they said. Leave nothing out. You won't remember it later. Your people fill out reports of where they went, who they talked to, what was said. You review every report. They miss something, you send them back out and get the answer."

The chief frowned. "Sounds like a lot of work."

"It is."

"What would you do...if you were doing it?"

"Chief?" A different voice.

Daniels and Asa turned to see an officer holding up a leather belt. His name tag said T. GREENE. "Found this behind the washer."

"So?"

"That could be used to strangle someone, Chief," Asa said. "Could be the murder weapon."

"Of course," Daniels said. "Uh...bag it, Tim. Could be fingerprints or DNA or some stuff like that on it."

The cop cast a glance at Asa and nodded before walking away.

"All right," Daniels said. "We'll start there. We need to see if that belt is the murder weapon."

"Don't rush, Chief. Slow it down and look at the facts and go from there."

Daniels didn't look confident, but he nodded and walked toward the stairway.

Asa was finally alone. He stared at the cross again for a long moment before returning to his office. The police would handle it; that was what they did. His job was to tend to the affairs of his church.

CHAPTER SIX

INTERROGATION

ASA SAT BEHIND HIS DESK. KYLE SAT ON ONE of the chairs in front, twirling a pen nervously through his fingers, while Mae and Jackie sat on the sofa. Jackie seemed a little nervous, while Mae's posture indicated that that elderly lady had not a care in the world.

Chief Daniels's large frame filled the doorway.

"Now I have to ask some questions," he said.

"Make this quick, Ned," Mae said. "I have things to do."

"How well did you know the deceased?"

"I didn't," Mae answered.

"She ever wait on you at the diner?"

"I haven't eaten at that place in three months, Ned."

"Mae, can you pick a lock?"

The elderly woman stood up. "Ned Daniels, I am seventy-five years old. If you think I killed that girl, you're nuttier than I gave you credit for." She walked out of the office, mumbling under her breath.

"Can anyone here pick a lock?"

"Depends on the lock," Asa said.

Daniels raised an eyebrow. "Huh?"

"Different kinds of locks, Chief. Lots of degrees of difficulty in picking them. Harder ones require lots of practice and skill."

"Sounds like you know a lot about them."

"Enough to know that if anyone in this office, including myself, would try to pick that lock, we'd probably still be at it. It would have been easier to use a key if we had one."

"Unless you're trying to make me think that," Daniels scribbled something in his notebook. Asa didn't know what it could be.

"What about you?" he asked Jackie.

"Can't pick a lock, Chief."

"Where were you last night?"

"Home. In bed with my husband."

"Any witnesses?"

Jackie stared at him. "My husband."

Daniels wrote something, then turned his attention to Kyle. "What about you?"

"Home all night. Not married, just my dog."

"So, no witnesses."

"But I can't pick a lock, either."

"So you say," Daniels said.

Asa rubbed his temple with thumb and forefinger.

"Problem there, Pastor?"

"Just a dead body in my church, Chief."

"Who gave you your keys?"

"Mae. This morning."

Daniels scribbled more in his notebook. "So, if you had killed her, you would have had to have picked it."

"That's right."

Daniels looked up. "Yeah. Right. Okay, that's all for now. Don't anyone leave town without checking with me."

"We'll do our best," Asa assured him.

When the front door closed, Asa sighed. "I think I might have a migraine."

Mae appeared in the doorway, one hand on her hip while the other hand held a folder. Her eyes flashed in annoyance. "Asa..."

"What now?"

"What was all of that?"

"Not sure. I think he was trying to interrogate us in hopes one of us had killed the girl." He paused. "I think."

"What did I tell you earlier?"

Asa's head was in his hands, heels of his palms resting on his eyes. "You told me."

"Asking me if I killed that poor girl, I should've smacked him upside his head for that." She cast a glance at Kyle. The young pastor met that piercing gaze for a moment before excusing himself. Mae sat down on the sofa.

"You all right?" she asked Asa.

"Yeah. Seeing something like that brings back some not-too-fond memories."

"He can't do this by himself," she said.

"You've told me that."

"So—?"

"Mae, I'm honored at your confidence in me, but I don't do homicides anymore. I'm a pastor, and have been for over twenty years. I'm afraid I'd be a little rusty at the detective thing."

She snorted. "Couldn't be worse than Ned Daniels. He's as dumb as last year's bird's nest."

"Policemen are a proud lot, Mae," Asa said. "They don't like interference, even from other policemen. I'm new in town, and I'd rather not step on the law's toes."

"It's your choice, of course, Pastor," Mae said. "But you might come to regret it."

"I hope you're wrong."

The elderly woman nodded. "Me too." She put the folder in front of him. "Time for church business."

Asa nodded. "Let's have it." He hoped Mae was wrong. He hoped he wouldn't regret not helping Ned.

CHAPTER SEVEN

THE MAYOR IS CONCERNED

NED DANIELS RAN A HAND THROUGH HIS hair and looked at the notebook where he'd scribbled things since arriving at the church. Half of them, he hated to admit now, he couldn't read, and some of the ones that he could made no sense.

What have I gotten into here?

That preacher seemed to know a lot about this stuff. Daniels couldn't imagine working murders in a big city. He'd heard that detectives elsewhere juggled multiple cases at once. The thought nearly gave Daniels a headache. His men were honest and hard-working, and they believed in the job, but was that enough to help him out with this?

A knock broke him away from his thoughts. Carla Reed stood in the door. "You wanted to see me, Chief?"

"Did you get all the evidence tagged and locked up?"

"Greene and I did it, yes, sir."

"Your thoughts on the case?"

Reed hesitated. "Took someone strong, I think."

"What happened with you and the victim?"

"She'd applied for a job at the diner. Gave the motel as her address. She had a prison record. Marty wanted me to check her out, see if she had any other secrets. I ran a basic background check. Clean since she got out. So I told Marty it was up to him if he wanted to hire her, but I was a little tentative about it, with her not having a more permanent address."

"You said you had some words with her?"

Reed shrugged. "Nothing big. She saw me coming out and asked me if I was checking up on her, you know, an ex-con and all."

"And what happened?"

"I told her no, that she was welcome here as long as she kept her nose clean."

Daniels seemed satisfied. "Okay. I was thinking. You have a class C license from the state, as far as your training goes."

"Yes, sir."

"Not much to it. Some classroom work, a little firearms training, and such. I'd like you to get more. You're a good candidate for the Academy, I think."

"Really?"

"Why not? You've proven yourself. Paperwork at my end will take weeks and then getting you scheduled for the nearest class cycle, but I'd like to see you put your paperwork together."

She smiled. "I'd like that, Chief."

He handed her a packet. "Here you go." He gestured at the clock. "Time for your shift to end. Go home, Carla."

"Thanks, Chief." She turned and came face to face with the mayor.

Mayor Ron Foster had once been a teacher in the county before running for office. No one had given him a substantial challenge since then. He gave a curt nod. "Officer Reed."

"Hello, Mr. Mayor," Carla said and moved past him and out the door.

Foster shut the door behind him.

Get ready, Daniels thought. "Mr. Mayor."

"What's this I hear about a murder, Ned?"

News traveled fast in a small town. "We're on it, Mr. Mayor."

"I also hear it happened in Grace Gospel Church."

"That's right."

"New pastor there, too."

"Yes, sir."

"Did you meet him?"

"Yes, sir. Dr. Asa Carter."

"What's your impression of him?"

"Smart man. He used to be a cop."

"A cop?"

"Yes, sir. His wife is from here, but he's from Chicago."

"Odd," Foster said. "New guy comes in and we get our first murder in years."

"I—I don't think he did it."

"Well, who did?"

"I don't know, sir. Yet."

Foster leaned against the doorframe. "Better find out soon, Ned. Girl comes into town, gets a job, and ends up dead a month later. Not good for our town's image."

"Sir, if you're that concerned, I can bring in the state—"

"No." Foster waggled a finger. "No state cops. They just get way too nosy in stuff. You're the chief, Ned. Get this thing solved. You. That pastor doesn't need to be nosing around."

"He might be useful to us, Ron," Daniels said.

Foster gave him a warning look and walked out. Daniels sighed.

Greene stuck his head in. "You okay, Chief?"

Daniels nodded. "Yeah. What is it?"

"You said you talked to the office staff at the church, right?"

"Yeah."

"There's one you didn't talk to," Greene said.

CHAPTER EIGHT

A TURN FOR THE WORSE

"I CAN'T BELIEVE IT," ELLEN SAID AS SHE SET the plate in front of her husband. Dinnertime had sometimes become a simple affair since Katy had moved out, but tonight Asa had been surprised by meatloaf and potatoes—his favorite. He looked at the plate.

"To what do I owe this?"

"It's been a rough day," Ellen said. "I thought you deserved it."

"Thanks."

"Don't thank me too much," she said. "I got out late because of a meeting, so I stopped off at the diner and picked it up."

"Well, it's thoughtful of you anyway." He leaned over and kissed her cheek. "Thank you."

Grace was said, and they ate in silence. Finally, Ellen said "I can't believe that someone was killed in the church."

"It's definitely a first in my ministry," Asa agreed.

"I'd seen her just the other day. She waited on me when I

stopped by for lunch. Kathy—she's a biology teacher—she and I had a quick lunch there during our planning day."

"One of the officers did a background check on her, on behest of the diner owner."

"Marty," Ellen said. "I think he's the owner."

"Right. So, an ex-con with a wild look for this town comes in and manages to get a job at a diner."

"Maybe she was trying to start over," Ellen suggested. "She wouldn't be the first one to do that."

Asa nodded. "I thought the same thing. If that's true, it's a shame it was cut short." He didn't notice Ellen's glance in her husband's direction.

"You're getting that look in your eye again," she said.

"What look?"

"That look you used to get when you got a particularly interesting case."

"It definitely has some peculiar aspects."

"Want to talk to me about it?"

Asa nodded. His wife remembered his homicide days. "Well, we know a little about her, where she was working. Okay, that's step one. Someone picked the lock to get in. Also, there was no mention of a car being left there that night. So, she didn't drive."

"Or the killer drove her car," Ellen suggested. "I hear Daniels is a good man."

"But not experienced at homicides," Asa said. "I don't want to step on toes. Mae seems to think I'm the only chance to solve the case."

"Do you want to do that?" Ellen asked. "Your eyes say yes."

Asa paused eating and stared at his plate. "I don't know. I'm angry that someone has been killed in my church, and I'm not sure the cops can solve it, and yet I don't know about..."

"You?"

"It's been a long time, honey. Don't know if I still have the chops."

"Did you pray about it?"

"Yeah. No bolt from the blue yet."

"Maybe," Ellen said, "it'll be something else."

They were doing dishes when the phone rang. Ellen took it, and Asa saw her face pale slightly. She put a hand over the mouthpiece and looked at her husband.

"It's Mae. Daniels and his men are at Walter's place. They're questioning him, and he's freaking out."

Asa sighed. "Tell her I'm on my way."

It took him two minutes to drive to the church, where three police cars sat in the parking lot, lights flashing. An officer Asa didn't know pointed toward Walter's apartment. Before he got there, Chief Daniels came out the door, visibly agitated.

"Chief, what's going on?"

"I went to talk to your janitor, and he had a meltdown on me, that's what. Reed is in there now, trying to calm him down."

"You should know better than that, Chief. You should have called me first."

"You have no business in it," Daniels growled and walked past.

Asa moved past him and went up the stairs to the door. He walked in to find Walter on the sofa, rocking back and forth. Carla Reed was trying to calm him.

"Walter..."

The janitor looked at him. His eyes were red and he was making a strange noise from his throat that sounded like a deep moan. "Pastor..."

"Officer Reed, can you give me a minute? Wait at the door, please."

She looked at Walter and back at Asa. "He was worse earlier."

Asa sat down and gave the cop a reassuring nod before turning back to the janitor. "Walter, calm down. It's okay."

"The police are here!"

"Yes. Do you remember the girl who was killed?"

"But I didn't kill her!"

Asa nodded. "I know. But Walter, Chief Daniels has to talk to everyone who works here at the church. Even Doc Adams. Mae, too."

"Mae couldn't have killed her."

"But he still had to talk to her. And he has to talk to you, too."

"I'm scared, Pastor. I want to go to bed."

"In a while, Walter. Do you want to see Mae?"

"Yes."

"Okay, you sit there and calm down. I'll fetch Mae, okay? Then we can talk to Chief Daniels together." He got up and walked outside. "Officer Reed, can you summon Mae? She's as close to a mom as he has. Once she calms him down..."

"Already on her way," Reed said. "She'll be here shortly."

Asa nodded his appreciation. "I've been told you see Walter a lot."

"I come by, usually when I do a security check of the church. If he's around, I say hi, sometimes bring him a pie or an angel food cake."

"Very thoughtful of you."

She glanced at the door. "I feel sorry for the guy. He has no one except his church family now, and he lives in this bubble that they've made for him."

"And you guys charged in and broke that bubble," Asa said.

"Just trying to do our job, Rev."

He paused. Mae, despite her age, marched up the flight of stairs. From the look on her face, Asa was sure she was ready to punch someone. She marched into Walter's apartment and shut the door.

"What now?" Carla Reed asked Asa.

"I guess we wait," he said. "Got any cake with you?"

"No, sorry."

"Pity," Asa sighed. He thought of his dinner on the dining table, getting cold.

CHAPTER NINE

WALTER IS QUESTIONED

MAE SAT ON THE SOFA. HER HAND LOOKED TINY resting on Walter's, but the janitor seemed calmer. She gave Asa a hard stare, and he decided this would have to be handled delicately. He sat down on Walter's other side and gave him a reassuring hug. Daniels stood in the doorway, a slight scowl on his face that Asa thought might not do anything to calm Walter down.

"Did Mae talk to you?" Asa asked.

Walter nodded. His eyes were red, and he sniffed a little.

"Can I ask you some questions?" Asa began.

"I—I guess."

"Tell me about your day yesterday. What did you do?"

"Well, I worked."

"I know. What time did you get up?"

"Seven. I have to be here by eight."

"What did you do when you got up?"

"Well. I showered, shaved, got dressed. I ate breakfast, put my bowl in the sink."

Asa nodded. "Okay. Then you went to work?"

Walter nodded. "I worked—I talked to you and Pastor Kyle."

"What time did you leave work?"

"Five."

"Then what?"

"I came home. I fixed dinner, and watched TV."

"What did you watch?"

"Cartoons. I like cartoons."

Asa gave him a reassuring pat on the shoulder. "What time did you go to bed?"

"Ten. I always go to bed at ten when I have to work."

"The girl. She worked at the diner. Had wild-colored hair and tattoos. Did you ever see her?"

His eyes widened. "It was Miss Tara?"

"You knew her?"

"She served me a lot when I went to the diner lately. I go there sometimes to eat. I like their chicken," he said. "She was nice to me." He looked at Asa, his eyes welling up. "Why would someone kill her?"

"That's what the police have to find out," Asa answered. He reached out, and Daniels handed him the bag with the belt found at the crime scene. "Walter, does this belt look familiar?"

Walter looked at it. "Looks like one of mine. Why is it in a bag?"

"How many do you have?"

"I have three like that."

"Where are they?"

"I'm wearing one." He pulled up his polo shirt to show the black belt in the loops of his jeans. "The others are hanging in my closet."

"Let's go see and count them, okay?" Asa said. "Chief Daniels is gonna go with us so it's official."

Asa, Mae, and the chief followed Walter into the tiny bedroom, and Walter pointed at the closet. "They're hanging up in there."

"Two of them?"

He nodded.

Daniels pulled some clothes aside. Asa looked in, and his heart sank.

"Walter, I only see one."

Walter's face screwed up in an almost comical expression. "One?" He looked in and then started looking frantically around the closet. "No, there should be two."

"Then this could be the missing belt."

"I—I guess it is, Pastor. Can I have it back?"

"Soon, but not yet."

Asa watched with a pit forming in his stomach as Daniels checked the label on the inside of the belt against the one in the closet. They were a match. Mae looked quickly into the closet, but found nothing.

"Walter, the belt in the bag was found in the baptistry storage room near where Tara was killed. Why did you have your belt up there?"

"I didn't. I was wearing one, and two were in my closet."

"But it wasn't. It was in the baptistry. How did it get up there?"

"I don't know."

"Did you put it in the washer or dryer? Or maybe you changed clothes and forgot about it or something?"

"No, Pastor Asa, I didn't."

Daniels was walking around the room. Looking. Asa gave the chief credit for that. He'd have done the same thing.

Criminals sometimes left evidence out in plain sight; and although Asa didn't believe for a moment that Walter Pence had killed the girl, the chief could not afford to be so biased.

"Did you put it up there earlier? Maybe sometime last week or so and forgot about it?"

"No." Walter's voice showed signs that he was stressing. "Am I in trouble?"

"If you left the church at five, did you go back later?"

"No."

"Are you sure?"

"Yes, Pastor, I am." Walter said. "I'm in trouble, aren't I?"

"No," Asa answered. "It's just a puzzle, and I'm trying to help you figure it out."

"I don't like puzzles," Walter said.

"Pastor?" Chief Daniels's voice.

Asa looked over to see Daniels holding a thin gold bracelet.

"Where'd you find that?"

"On the dresser."

"Walter, what is that?" Asa asked.

Walter Pence turned and looked at the bracelet in the cop's hand. "I don't know."

"It's a bracelet, Walter. Like a woman wears."

He nodded. "My momma used to wear one."

"Is this the one she wore?"

"No," he answered. "She was...buried with hers."

"So, whose is it?"

"I don't know."

"Where did you get it?" Asa asked.

"I don't know. I've never seen it before."

"It was here on the dresser, Walter," Daniels said. "'Fess up, boy. That dead girl was missing a bracelet, and here one comes up and lands on your dresser. You tellin' me you don't know nothing about it?"

"No, sir, I don't know!" Walter's eyes widened. "I don't know!"

"Walter." Mae's voice was a calm contrast to the rising tone of Walter's denial. "Tell me. You've always been able to tell me anything, right?"

He nodded. "Yes, ma'am."

"Where did you get the bracelet?"

"I never got a bracelet, Ms. Mae. I don't know how it got there."

"Walter, tell me the truth."

"Ms. Mae, I am. I've never told a fib to you. Ever."

Daniels called out and Carla Reed came in. She put the bracelet in an evidence bag. She looked at Asa.

"Make sure everything is filled out right," Daniels said.

"Yes, sir." Reed nodded and left.

Chief Daniels walked over and put a hand on Walter's broad shoulder. "It gives me no pleasure, Pastor, to do this. Walter Pence, you're under arrest for the murder of Tara Brooks."

CHAPTER TEN

A DECISION IS MADE

ASA RETURNED TO HIS OFFICE AND HEARD Mae rustling papers and banging drawers closed. He walked out to find her sitting at her desk like a sentinel. She'd done the same thing for decades now, watching over this church and those who helped lead it.

"Go home, Mae, if you want to. Take the day off."

She stared at the wall. "I've known him since he was a baby," she said. "I watched his mama struggle with raising him and people talking about them. It was never easy for either of them."

"I imagine not."

"She got sick and didn't want Walter to know. He came to me one day and asked me flat out if his mama was going to die. She was bad off by then, almost bedridden."

"What did you tell him?"

She frowned. "I searched my mind and heart and did some praying in that moment, Pastor, I'll tell you. And I figured it this way. When she was gone, I'd be the closest thing to a mama that he had. And I wouldn't lie to him. So, I told him." She pulled a tissue from the drawer and daubed her eyes. "You think he killed that girl?"

"Mae, it's not my place—"

"It *is* your place. You're his pastor now. He already looks up to you, though you've only just got here. And there's your experience. You've talked to the guilty before."

"I have. And the innocent."

"You think he killed that girl?"

"I wouldn't want to start off our relationship by lying," Asa said. "I don't know."

"Well, I know. Walter Pence couldn't hurt a fly," Mae said.

"What about the bracelet? The belt?"

"He didn't kill that girl!" Mae said, and a sob choked her words. "I know it." She straightened and took a deep breath. "Trust me, Asa, I know that boy."

He stared at her for what seemed a long time, though it was only a second or two. "I haven't done this sort of thing in two decades, Mae."

"I know."

"I'm going to trust you," he said. "Is there an attorney in the congregation?"

"Yes. A good one."

"Think he'd represent Walter? First appearance won't be until Monday."

Mae nodded. "He'll do it."

"You sound so sure."

"He's my son-in-law," Mae said. "He'll do it."

"Get on it, then," Asa said.

She smiled. "I already have."

WHILE IT WAS NOT UNUSUAL FOR ASA TO BE silent at dinner, it was another thing for him to be silent all evening. He left the table, and a half hour later Ellen found him in his study, elbows on the desk, his hands folded and against his forehead.

"What's wrong?"

"I'm afraid to tell you."

"Those are the first words you've uttered since you said grace."

"Sorry."

She walked over and put a hand on his shoulder and gave a small squeeze. "You want to help Walter."

It amazed Asa how well she knew him. He could only utter "I don't know how."

"Yes, you do."

"I'm scared, honey."

"There's nothing wrong with that."

"I haven't done this sort of thing in a long time."

"Kyle told me you read that crime scene, saw the cause, estimated the time of death—everything he knows from it, you gave him," she said. "Don't tell me you haven't got the skill."

"Honey, it was automatic. Like a reflex."

"Told you. You still have it."

"I don't feel like it."

"Do you think Walter killed her?"

"I don't know. I don't know him well enough yet. Mae says he couldn't have done it. Most of the congregation I talked to after service says the same thing."

"Maybe they're right."

"A conundrum for sure," Asa said. "If Walter did it, he wouldn't have had to pick the lock. He has a key." He shook his head. "No pieces to this puzzle yet."

"Could they railroad him to jail? I hate to think the chief would do such a thing."

Asa shrugged. "Mae's son-in-law is an attorney. She says he'll be Walter's counsel."

"Thank God."

"If he's innocent, then there is a killer loose."

"He needs to be found," Ellen said.

Asa got up and grabbed his jacket.

"Where are you going?"

"To ask Walter a question," Asa said. A moment later, the front door closed. He never saw the slight smile on his wife's face.

CHAPTER ELEVEN

ASA GETS AN ANSWER

ASA WAS ALMOST TO HIS CAR WHEN KYLE pulled into the drive. The young minister was visibly upset.

"He couldn't have killed that girl."

"So I've been told."

"Well, we have to do something," Kyle said.

"I am. Mae's son-in-law is going to represent him. I'm going to talk to the chief."

"What about me?"

"You've known Walter longer than I have."

"A month, maybe."

"Nevertheless, he's entitled to pastoral visits. Go visit him. Calm him down, explain that we're going to do everything we can to get him out. Do you know Mae's son-in-law?"

"Sure. Name's Kevin."

"If Kevin is there talking to him, leave them alone unless Kevin says otherwise. Got it?"

"Yeah. What are you talking to the chief about?"

"I'll think of something," Asa said.

Asa found the chief in his office, feet on his desk and basking in the self-congratulatory glow cops had sometimes from catching the bad guy. A large mug of coffee sat within reach, and Daniels grinned when he saw Asa.

"Ah, Reverend. Here to see the prodigal son?"

Asa jerked a thumb toward Kyle, who was still with him before going next door to the jail. "*He* is. Is counsel present?"

Daniels shook his head. "Nah, he's been here and gone. Mae must have called him instantly. He almost beat us here to the station. I've seen him several times; never dealt with him, though. He was rather agitated."

"I'm sure," Asa said. He turned to Kyle, who hesitated before giving a nod. Kyle left for the jail.

Daniels waited until the young minister was gone before turning to Asa. "The mayor was here earlier. Wants you to keep your nose out of it."

"Why would he want that?"

"I'm afraid I don't quite know," Daniels replied.

"What about you?"

"I'm afraid...I don't quite know."

"Chief, I think there's a killer out there and it's not Walter Pence."

Daniels grunted. "You think the boy's innocent?"

"Don't know him that well. Mae says he is. So does Kyle."

"Mae would. Known him all his life. People have a hard time accepting that the ones they love can do bad things."

"Your case against him is circumstantial."

"The belt, the bracelet, plus he had access," Daniels said. "Pretty convincing."

"But not motive," Asa said. "Why would he kill the girl?"

Daniels spread his hands. "Who knows? Maybe it was an impulse thing, you know. A crime of passion."

"There's no hint he was interested in her like that."

"Maybe he was and just hasn't confessed," the chief said.

"Have you questioned him further?"

"What's to question? The evidence points to him. He had access to both the church and the baptistry."

"So why would he have picked the lock?"

"To throw me off the trail." Daniels tapped his forehead.

"What about the bracelet?"

"What about it?"

"How do you know it's her bracelet?"

"Why wouldn't it be?"

"Can you prove that it's hers?"

"Well...not exactly."

"Your case is circumstantial at best," Asa said. "Chief, I want a favor. Let me talk to Walter. I only need a couple of minutes, and you can come with me if you want. Depending on what he says, I'm going to make a decision."

"About what?"

"About whether or not you have the wrong man."

"I don't think I do."

"We shall see."

Daniels waved a hand. He didn't like this know-it-all coming in to question his decisions, but he had to admit that the preacher knew his stuff. He'd read the crime scene better than anyone Daniels knew. But he felt confident in his accusations about Walter Pence. The guy was as guilty as they come. "Help yourself."

Asa found Kyle talking to Walter in his cell. When Asa appeared, Walter saw him, and his face went pale. "Pastor Asa?"

"Hi, Walter. How are you doing?" The jailer opened the door and Asa stepped in. Asa put a gentle hand on the big man's shoulder. "We're doing everything we can to get you out of here."

Walter nodded. "Pastor Kyle told me. I didn't kill her."

"I know."

"Really?"

"Really. I do." Asa sat on the bunk beside him. "Walter, did you ever play 'pretend' when you were a kid?"

"Oh, sure. I played astronaut."

"Sounds like fun."

"Yeah. I would pretend I was on the moon or on Mars. I could even walk kinda bouncy, like the guys on the moon do."

Kyle was looking at Asa with an expression of confusion. Where was the pastor going with this? Asa nodded reassuringly as though saying he had a plan.

"I need you to pretend for me, Walter. It's very important."

"Okay."

"Now, we know you didn't kill that girl, but pretend that you did."

"But I didn't—"

Asa held out a hand. "I know, but let's pretend you did. You wanted to kill her and you decided to take her into the baptistry and strangle her with your belt. What would you do next?"

"What do you mean?"

"Walter, the woman was killed with your belt, left at the scene, and a woman's bracelet that might be hers was found in your place. That's a serious thing. I need to know if you can tell me anything that might help me prove that you didn't do this."

Walter shook his head, his eyes welling. "I can't think, Pastor. I'm slow, you know."

"How many people have keys to your place?"

"Just me. And Mae."

"No one else?"

"No."

"Anyone ever come by and see you?"

"Lots. Mae, of course, and several ladies from the church. Miss Kay and Miss Jane, and Miss Elaine. They always bring me food. Officer Greene and Miss Carla, they both see me sometimes when they're on patrol."

"Officer Reed?"

"Yeah. She gives me cakes. The lemon ones. I like lemon."

"What about Officer Greene?"

"He comes by to say hi, make sure I'm okay."

"Anyone else?"

"Well, Bill, the maintenance guy, sometimes. I had a sink problem last week, and he came over and fixed it."

"Does he have a key?"

"No. I offered to get him one, but he said that it was my place and he respected my privacy. Or something like that."

Asa paused. So far, he had nothing much to go on.

"All right, Walter. You've seen Mr. Kevin?"

Walter nodded. "Yes, he came to see me."

"You do exactly as he tells you, okay?"

"I will."

Asa got up. "I'll see you tomorrow."

He'd gotten to the cell door when Walter said, "I wouldn't have done that."

Asa and Kyle turned. "Done what?" Kyle asked.

"If I'd killed that girl, I wouldn't have left my belt there and took her bracelet to my place," Walter said. He looked up. "That would be stupid."

Asa smiled. "Thanks, Walter."

Daniels was still in his office in nearly the same position as when Asa had left. This time, the chief had a cup of coffee.

"Find out what you needed to know?" Daniels asked between sips.

"I did," Asa answered. "Did you check the motel?"

Daniels furrowed his brow. "Motel?"

"Chief, Tara was living in the motel. I want to look at her room."

"Why?"

"Because the more you can find out about someone, the easier it can be to find out who had the means or motive to kill them."

"I have the murderer. He's big enough to have done it, and let's face it, Pastor, he's not the sharpest tool in the shed."

"But smart enough to know better than to leave the murder weapon at the scene," Asa said. "You coming, or do you want me to do it without the police?"

Daniels sighed and swung his feet off the desk. He'd planned on an early lunch. "Okay. Let's do it your way."

CHAPTER TWELVE

THE ROOM

ASA REALIZED IT WAS THE FIRST TIME HE'D been in a police car in a long time. He remembered his training phase, riding with an old sergeant who had taken a scared kid out of the Academy and taught him how to be a cop.

There was only one motel in Glen Pines. The Glen Pines Motel was a single-story L-shaped building on the outskirts of town. It had few amenities, but it was clean and had a decent restaurant. Daniels walked into the office, with Asa right behind him. A young brunette was behind the desk. "Hey, Chief."

"Morning, Liz. What room was Tara Brooks staying in?"

"You know that's private."

"She's dead, Liz, so she can't give her consent."

"You have a warrant?"

"We don't need one," Asa said.

She looked at the pastor. "Who are you?"

"Reverend Carter," Asa said.

"How do you know you don't need one?"

"Liz!" came a booming female voice from the back office. "Give Ned whatever he needs."

"Yes, ma'am," Liz said.

Daniels hollered toward the office. "Thank you, Gail!"

A rotund older woman waddled out of the office. She gave a curious glance at Asa. "Trouble, Chief?"

"Just routine, Gail."

"You talking about poor Tara?"

"Who else would I be talking about, Gail, unless you got another dead guest?"

"A crying shame." Gail went to the antiquated computer on the desk. "Checked in six weeks ago Monday. Paid in cash for a week, made regular payments afterwards."

"We need to have a look," Daniels said.

Liz handed him the key. Asa could tell she didn't want to.

Housekeeping had come through and cleaned the room. The bed was made, fresh towels hung from the racks, and more lay folded neatly on the shelf in the bathroom. Asa opened the small refrigerator to find a six-pack of soda and some slices of cheese and lunch meats. A half loaf of white bread waited on the table beside it. A small hot plate, unplugged, was on the counter. A potted geranium sat on the windowsill.

"She wasn't eating out much," Daniels said. He looked at the open suitcase lying on the floor by the bed. He opened a pocket inside the suitcase and pulled out a small wad of cash. "Look-ee here."

"How much?"

Daniels counted. "One hundred fifty-three."

"Probably from tips," Asa said. "I hear she did well." He made a mental note to talk to her boss. He went over to the plant and looked it over.

"You like geraniums, Pastor?"

"Uh-huh."

They spent a while combing through her suitcases. Tara had taken the liberty of hanging a few things up in the tiny closet. They found nothing of interest, and Daniels straightened up with a sigh. "Told you. Waste of time."

The mirror caught Asa's eye. He went to it.

"You see something?" Daniels called out. The chief walked over and squinted at the three photographs stuck into the space between the mirror and frame.

"Photos," Asa said.

"I can see that," Daniels said. "What's so fascinating?"

Asa stepped back and looked closely.

"What?"

"Notice anything odd about them, Chief?"

Daniels put his fist to his chin and stared. "Not really. They show our victim. From the background I'd say it was in Kentucky." He pointed to one photo. It showed two young girls together standing on a dirt road with wooded mountains behind them. It wasn't hard to pick out Tara Brooks. Even at that young age, her hair was streaked with purple, the colors now faded along with the rest of the photo.

"Wonder who that is," Daniels said. "Friend?"

"Probably. Maybe her best friend. Or a sibling. There's a big space between the top one there…" Asa pointed, "…to the next one."

"So?"

Asa bent down and breathed hard on the space between two of the pictures. His breath on the mirror revealed an outline.

Daniels leaned forward. "There was another picture there in the space."

"Yes. There's a photo missing."

"Is it around here?"

"Haven't found it if it is."

"Someone took it," Daniels said. "The deceased, maybe?"

"Maybe," Asa agreed. "But she put it up there with the others. Seems odd that it would be missing."

"Maybe she stuck it there and it fell off, got damaged, and she tossed it. Maid's already been through here, so you can kiss any idea of finding it goodbye." Daniels took a second and stepped to the phone and called the front desk.

"When was this room last visited by housekeeping? And before that?" He put his hand over the phone. "Housekeeping came in yesterday and straightened up. Came in this morning and saw nothing had been touched, so they left it."

Asa took the phone. Daniels watched, interested. "Did the same person visit the room both days? Is she working? Good. Could you send her up, please? Thanks." He hung up.

"What are you doing?"

"Confirming our theory," Asa answered. "I hope."

The maid's name was Hetta, and she had been employed at the motel for nearly ten years. She was a slender Black woman. She sat fidgeting on the edge of the bed.

"What's this all about, Chief?"

"Have you been handling this room since Ms. Brooks came in?"

"I handle all the rooms, Chief. Ain't got but ten in the whole motel."

"Did you ever see Ms. Brooks?"

"Once or twice. Polite and respectful, which surprised me. All those tattoos and everything. Even gave me a tip once."

"When was this?"

"First day she was here."

Asa stepped in. "Did you notice the photos on the mirror?"

"Sure. But there's one missing. There were four of them."

"Are you sure?" Daniels asked.

"Sure, Chief, I can count. Only three there now."

"Do you remember what the missing photo was?"

"Nothing much. Two teenagers, one of them looked like her. Arms around each other like friends do."

"Do you know the other girl in the picture?" Asa asked.

"Not a clue," Hetta said and looked around. "She ain't been here recently. Nothing's been touched—'cept the picture, of course."

"When was the last time you saw her?"

"Wednesday. Came by to service the room. She was on her phone, talking to someone. Saw me and told me to come by later."

"And you don't know who she was talking to?"

"Of course I don't. How would I know that, Chief?"

"Maybe she mentioned a name," Asa suggested.

"No, nothing. Say, what is this about?"

"She's dead," Daniels said. "Murdered."

Hetta covered her mouth. "Oh, Lordy..."

They let the shaken woman go, and Daniels sighed. "Wonder what happened to that picture."

"Did you find a motel key on her?" Asa asked.

Daniels froze and cocked his head. "No."

"How was she going to get back into her room?"

"Maybe she'd lost it. Get another from the front desk."

"Or...?"

Daniels grimaced. "Or her killer took it."

CHAPTER THIRTEEN

ASA TALKS TO THE BOSS

MAE WAS SO EXCITED, ASA COULD BARELY understand her through the phone. "Pastor, they've released Walter, thank God."

"They didn't charge him?"

"No. I told you Kevin knew his stuff." She paused. "And thanks to you."

"That's good news," Asa said.

"The judge says he's not to leave town, although he never goes anywhere anyway."

"Do what you need to do to get him settled back in, and I'd like to see him back to work tomorrow."

"He'd love that," Mae said and hung up. Asa gave a silent prayer of thanksgiving before he walked into the diner.

Martin "Marty" Plumley could trace his roots back to the founding of Glen Pines. The local cemetery had a sign in honor of his great-great grandfather, who had come here in the 1800s and helped found the small village that became the town. The

Red Oak Diner had been the dream and love of his mother, and Marty had carried the legacy onward. Although proud of his heritage, he was oddly loath to attach the family name to any of their endeavors.

Marty was a stocky fellow who did not look like he had trained in culinary arts in Philadelphia, but he had worked hard to learn his craft with the express aim of coming back to take over his mother's restaurant. He still had his white apron on when he met Asa in the corner booth near the kitchen entrance.

"I tell you, Pastor, I'm in shock," he said. "I admit, I had my doubts about her when I first hired her. I mean, the hair and all the tattoos. But she was one of the best workers I ever had. Hard-working, friendly with the guests, and got a lot of tips."

"Did you ask why she'd come here to Glen Pines?"

He nodded. "I did. She said she'd done her time and she knew how hard it would be for her to start over back home, so she wanted somewhere fresh to try to get back on her feet. Promised me that if I took the chance, I wouldn't be sorry." He smiled. "She was very persuasive; I'll say that for her."

"I heard you had the cops check up on her."

Marty gave a slight nod. "I had Carla just run a check on her, make sure her story checked out and that she hadn't gotten into any trouble since getting out."

"How did Tara feel about that?"

He shrugged. "Fine, I guess. Never talked to me about it."

"Was she dating anyone?"

"I doubt that. Nothing serious, if she was. Besides, she took extra shifts, worked any time she could to make money. I did see her talking to your janitor a couple of times."

"Walter?"

"That's right. He came in a few times. I think he kind of liked her." He paused. "Come to think of it, I think she mentioned to one of the other girls that Walter had asked her out once."

"What did she say?"

"You'd have to ask Kay. She was kind of friendly with Tara."

"She here today?"

"No. She'll be in tomorrow, though."

"Where does she live?"

"That apartment building on Market. Not sure which one." He shook his head. "It's a shame, I'll tell you."

"When was the last time you saw her?"

"The night before. She worked closing for me and was anxious to get out. Wasn't like her."

"Did you ask why?"

"No, but her mind was definitely on something, and she wanted to get done and leave."

"Did she seem upset?"

"Not upset," Marty answered. "More like anxious."

Asa could only nod. "Did she ever have trouble with anyone?"

"Trouble?"

"Any arguments, irate customers, admirers who didn't like being rejected?"

He shook his head. "None that I know about. She was a hard worker and a good person, Reverend. It's not fair." He held up a finger. "That's the main argument I got against there being an Almighty. If there is one, he could make things fairer down here."

"Well," Asa said as he got up, "Jesus never said life would be fair. Thanks for your time."

"CHIEF?"

Daniels looked up to find Greene at his door. "What is it, Tim?"

"Sorry for just now telling you this, but the night that the girl was killed, I was doing a drive through the church parking lot and I saw someone walking alone through the lot."

"Who was it?"

"That girl from the flower shop. Violet."

"And she was alone?"

"Yes, sir."

"Well, did you stop and ask?"

"Of course, Chief, I stopped and asked her if she was okay and what in the world she was doing out walking after dark." Greene paused.

"And?"

"Oh, well, she said she was out for a stroll and was heading home."

"What time was this?"

"I'd have to check the patrol log, but about ten or eleven."

"And you thought to wait until now to tell me?"

"Well, I didn't know. Didn't think much of it. I don't think she killed that girl, Chief. She's a little mouse of a thing."

Daniels sighed. "Go get her. I want to talk to her for a minute."

"But I don't think—"

"Just get her, Tim, and next time how about you think of telling me these things when we're at the crime scene, rather than days later."

Greene swallowed. "Yes, sir."

Daniels waved him off. "Shoo."

Greene vanished out the door on his way to the flower shop. Daniels pressed the intercom button on the phone to the dispatcher. "Find the Reverend. Tell him I need him at the station."

"Right away, Chief."

Daniels took in a deep breath, let it out. A person seen in the parking lot of the church the night of the murder and no one told him. The mayor would have him roasting over a pit if he found out.

CHAPTER FOURTEEN

THE FRIEND

STONEBROOK APARTMENTS CONSISTED OF THREE tri-story brick buildings surrounding a tennis court and swimming pool. It took Asa nearly fifteen minutes to locate Kay Ralton's apartment. A tousle-headed sleepy brunette answered the door in a T-shirt that Asa found almost too short for comfort.

"Kay?"

She rubbed her eyes. "No, I'm Cathy, her roommate. You are?"

"Reverend Asa Carter. I was wondering if I could speak to Kay for a moment."

"She's still sleeping, I think."

A voice from within sounded. "Who's at the door?"

"Some preacher wants to talk to you," Cathy called back.

"I already found God."

Asa leaned forward, speaking into the room. "Kay, I'm Reverend Carter. I'd like to talk to you about Tara Brooks."

There was a long pause, and Asa feared she would say no. "Cathy, let him in."

Like with most young people starting out, the furnishings were sparse and reminded Asa of his own journey when he'd gotten his first place. A couple of posters on the wall, a TV in the corner, and one floor lamp. He was shown to a threadbare sofa, and Cathy stood there for a moment. "Uh...would you like some water or somethin'?"

"I'm fine, thank you."

She walked off, the tee riding up a little, and Asa turned his studious attention to the floor until Kay appeared. She was a little brunette, pretty but not beautiful, and, unlike her roommate, had chosen to wear a white terry-cloth robe. She fiddled with the collar as though she feared it might open suddenly. Asa figured Cathy would not have been so concerned.

"I'm sorry about Cathy," Kay said. Her eyes were puffy. "She's not very modest when she should be."

Asa didn't know what to say to that, so he smiled. "Tell me about Tara."

"I can't believe it. She was a good person, Reverend."

"I talked to Marty. He said she was a hard worker."

"She was. She was wanting to save up some money. She'd lived at a halfway house before coming to Glen Pines, and she earned a little bit there. She'd gotten her motorcycle cheap and fixed it up." She smiled. "She was a smart, tough gal."

"Tara had a motorcycle?"

"Yeah, one of those sport ones, where you bend over to ride it."

"Any problems with anyone?"

"Not really. She was great with the customers."

"Were they all okay with her?"

"Well, you know this town. Small, and people set in their ways about how things should be. Girl comes along with her colored hair and tattoos, and some just can't accept it."

"Any time it got bad?"

"No. Just whispers and slight looks."

"How did Tara handle that?"

"Better than I would have. I think it stung her some, but she never let on."

"No arguments or threats?"

"Not from customers."

"What about anyone else?"

"Couple of guys hit on her, nothing serious, but there was Pat Cobb."

"Tell me about him."

"He came in the diner, saw Tara, and asked her out. She asked me about him, and I told her Cobb could be bad news. He had a record, and she had to keep her nose clean because the cops would be watching her a little closer than most, so she turned him down."

"How did he take that?"

"He wouldn't take no for an answer. The day before she died, I saw them arguing outside the diner."

"About what?"

"Tara came in mad. Said he wouldn't give it up, that she'd told him no and that was that."

"But Cobb didn't want to accept that?"

"Apparently not. I thought I heard Cobb say to her that he'd kill her."

"Are you sure?"

"Pretty sure. Sounded like it to me."

"Do you think he could have...?"

"He's not a nice guy, Reverend. And he was mad. Who knows?"

"I appreciate your time," Asa said. "Thank you for seeing me and for your help." He handed her his card. "If you think of anything, let me or Chief Daniels know."

"Actually, there was someone else. I saw Tara having a talk outside the flower shop one day. Looked pretty heated."

"With who?"

"Violet. She works there in the shop."

"You don't know what it was about?"

"Couldn't say," she said. "Sorry."

Asa was too.

CHAPTER FIFTEEN

ANOTHER PERSON IS QUESTIONED

ASA HAD WALKED FROM THE DINER TO THE apartment, and he was in the apartment building's parking lot when Carla Reed caught him. "There you are, Pastor. Chief wants to see you."

"How'd you find me?"

"Marty said you might be here," Carla said. "Come on." She radioed in to the dispatcher to let the chief know that Asa had been found and they were on their way.

He hopped in. For the second time in as many days, he was in a squad car. He caught a slight whiff of perfume. "What's going on?"

"Tim—Officer Greene—questioned a woman who was in your church parking lot the night of the murder."

"Who?"

She shrugged. "Not sure. I wasn't privy to all the details, just told to find you."

"Does Ned think she's a suspect?"

"Don't know that either. I think he wants you there to get your opinion."

They arrived at the station, and Daniels motioned Asa into his office where a small-framed woman sat meekly in one of the leather chairs in front of the desk. She was wearing a plain flowery dress and black loafers that were years out of date and that looked as uncomfortable as their owner.

"Pastor Carter, meet Violet Corbin."

"Hello, Violet," Asa said, smiling.

"I—I didn't do anything, Chief," Violet said in a high voice that matched her mousy demeanor.

Daniels waved her off. "The night when Doc Adams says Tara Brooks was killed, Officer Greene found Violet walking through the church parking lot. When was that, Violet? About eleven?"

"I don't know anything about that girl getting killed."

"Seems you've been in the church parking lot a lot lately," Daniels said. "Odd hours of the night."

"I don't sleep well," Violet said. "A walk helps me."

"You weren't scoping the church out, were you?"

"Ned..." Asa said.

"I don't know what that means," Violet said.

"Chief—" Asa motioned him aside. "You're a big guy and you're clearly scaring her. You'll never get anything out of her this way. How about letting me do a softer approach?"

"Ah, good cop, bad cop," Daniels said. "I like it." He glared at Violet and walked out, shutting the door behind him. Violet watched him go.

"He's not a nice man."

"Yeah, he gets a little worked up sometimes," Asa said. "Let's talk for a minute. Where do you work?"

She swallowed. “Am I under arrest?”

“No.” He pointed at her wrists. “That’s a nice bracelet.”

“Thank you.”

“Where’d you get it?”

“A friend got it for me.”

“A friend?”

“Yeah.” The word was drawn out a little.

“You like bracelets, Violet?”

“Yes, I do.”

“Where do you work?”

“Flower shop. I help Miss Mabel.”

“What do you do there?”

“Lots of things. Whatever she wants me to do.”

“You like working there?”

“Yes. Most of the time.”

“Most?”

“Sometimes Miss Mabel gets mean customers. I don’t like them.”

“Someone saw you having an argument with Tara Brooks a few days ago.”

She seemed to shrink, if that was possible for her small frame. “It was—it was a misunderstanding.”

“What was it?”

“I thought she had done something that she didn’t do, that’s all. We got it straightened out.”

“Ah,” Asa said. He’d wanted details, but her tone indicated that she might not tell him, so he decided to move on. “Violet, I know you didn’t kill that girl. I think you’re much too nice for that sort of stuff.”

“Thank you, Reverend. I never hurt anyone in my life.”

“Good to hear,” Asa said. “When you were there that

night taking a walk, did you see anything unusual? See anyone around?"

"No. No one. Except the police car and Officer Greene."

"He said he stopped you about eleven. Is that right?"

She nodded.

"When did you get home?"

"About eleven-fifteen. I only live a few blocks away. On Oak."

"You live alone?"

"Sort of. I rent a room."

"From whom?"

"The Bakers. They're nice people. They go to your church."

"And you're sure you didn't see or hear anything while you were there?"

"I thought I heard shouting," she said.

Asa leaned forward. "Shouting?"

"Yeah. Like arguing."

"From where?"

"I couldn't tell exactly. It was very faint."

"Could you make out any words?"

"No," she said. "Like I said, I wasn't sure I heard it, but I think I did."

"From inside the church?"

Violet Corbin paused, then slowly nodded. "Yes."

CHAPTER SIXTEEN

A VISIT TO COBB

"WHY DO YOU THINK SHE'S INNOCENT?" Daniels asked Asa.

They were in Daniels's police car on a two-lane blacktop. Behind them, Greene and another officer followed.

"Chief, that woman's so meek and mousy, she didn't do it."

"Maybe she's got another side to her."

"Maybe," Asa said. "I can't see her doing it, though."

"So, she was just there going for a walk?"

"Maybe." Silently, Asa thought, Maybe not.

"They said this Cobb threatened Tara Brooks?"

"According to her friend, she said she heard Cobb threaten her," Asa said. "You know this guy?"

"Yeah, we've met," Daniels said. "He's a real peach. Got a record for assault, burglary; did time for some of it."

As the city gave way to woods, Asa said "Chief, we're out of the city limits. Do you have jurisdiction out here?"

"Yes, since they passed a law giving it to me," Daniels said. "Sheriff's department is too far away, and he doesn't take law enforcement too seriously in this area. He prefers the other aspects of the job. I have the authority and can tap anyone I want to assist." He glanced over. "I am a little hesitant in taking you, though."

"I won't hold you responsible if I get shot," Asa said.

"Good. You stay in the car. Understood?"

"Roger that."

Pat Cobb lived in a ramshackle house on a wooded knoll overlooking a small stream. Used tires and a doorless refrigerator cluttered the front porch. A storage shed stood nearby, and a larger shed was at the end of the driveway. Asa resisted the urge to get out, but realized it was stupid. He had no badge, no firearm, and no authority. For a moment, he wished he had them. There were times he secretly missed the job, and now was one of them.

The officers spread out. Greene and the other officer took the back, while Daniels walked to the front door. He stood to the side and pounded. "Cobb! Chief Daniels here. I need to talk to you!"

Nothing.

Daniels pounded again. "Come on, Pat, your truck is here. We've got the house covered. Come on out."

Cobb appeared, but not at the door. He came out of the large shed, running headlong toward the cop cars, heading toward the pickup truck, near where Daniels had parked his car.

"Hey!" Daniels shouted, and the two officers left the porch and took off after the fleeing Cobb. Greene was faster than his boss and intercepted Cobb, almost stopping him, but the man spun away and shoved Greene to the ground.

The passenger-side door of Daniels's car flew open, clipping Cobb's right leg, turning him in mid-stride. He collided with the rear passenger door before falling onto the hard clay. He rolled and lay there stunned, his body refusing his mind's commands to get up and run. Daniels flipped the boy over and cuffed him. Once Cobb was secured, Daniels glanced over at Asa. "Did you do that?"

"Must have been a faulty latch," Asa said.

COBB SAT HANDCUFFED ON HIS SOFA. TWO bricks held up one corner of the couch, and there was a hole in one of the arms.

"Now, Paddy-boy," Daniels said. "Let's have a chat."

"I didn't do anything," Cobb said.

"Which is why you ran," Daniels said. He gestured to Asa. "This is Reverend Carter. So don't lie to me in front of God's servant."

Cobb looked at Asa. "You don't look like a reverend. You got cop eyes."

Daniels smiled. "See, Rev? Kid knows everything." He turned his attention back to the suspect. "Pat, I got people who say they heard you threaten Tara Brooks the day before she was murdered. Want to tell me about that?"

"No."

"Okay. I could have my boys go through all your stuff here. Wonder how much of it is on our stolen property list."

Cobb sighed. "I didn't kill her."

"You threatened her," Asa said. "People heard you say you were going to kill her."

"I got nothing to say to you."

"Well, I have you for assaulting a police officer, fleeing, and resisting arrest," Daniels said. "That'll do for now." He jerked a thumb toward the police cars. "Get him out of here."

Greene and another officer, who Asa learned was Miller, hustled the sulking Cobb out. Daniels looked around. "Wonder if we'd find any lockpick tools here."

"Maybe, but you want to expend man power to go through this dump?"

"What do you suggest?"

"Keep him in the brig for a while. Maybe we'll take another crack at him before you get a warrant."

"He won't say anything."

"Maybe not to you," Asa said.

Daniels smiled.

Greene and Miller were already en route to the station. Asa and the chief got into the car.

"Nice job back there."

"Caught a fleeing perp like that once before," Asa said.

Daniels grimaced. "Ouch."

CHAPTER SEVENTEEN

A CLUE IS FOUND?

ASA PULLED THE PHOTO HE'D TAKEN FROM Tara's motel room out of his desk drawer. It showed two young girls looking into the camera, two young smiling faces.

"What's that?" Kyle had appeared in the doorway.

"Took this from Tara's motel room."

"Why?"

"Don't know. Instinct mostly. Could be nothing."

Kyle smiled. "A clue?"

"I don't know yet."

The younger pastor's face fell slightly. Ever hopeful, he looked at the photo. "Looks like Tara."

"Yeah. Trying to figure out who the other girl is."

"Sibling? Best friend?"

"Either of them," Asa said. "Been pondering why she'd have them with her in her motel room on display like that."

"She got out of prison, maybe those were the only items from her past that she had."

"Maybe," Asa answered. "What was she doing here?" He stared at the photo and, sighing, put it back in his desk.

"Like you said, she was starting over."

"I want to believe that, but something is off."

"What?"

"I don't know, Kyle. I just don't know. Something doesn't..." Asa shook his head. "Maybe I've lost my touch." He stood.

"Where are you going?" Kyle asked.

"Has the baptistry been swept or touched since the murder?"

"No, I don't think so."

"Good. Let's see what we can find."

Kyle grinned. "Looking for clues. Oh, boy." He rushed down the hall, and Asa heard the opening of a cabinet. In a moment, Kyle appeared, still grinning, with a magnifying glass in his hand. "This might come in handy."

Asa suppressed a laugh. "Come on, Sherlock."

Silence greeted them when they stepped into what had been a crime scene. Asa glanced at the now-empty pool, and the image of Tara Brooks floating lifeless there flashed across his mind. He pushed it aside.

"What are we looking for?" Kyle asked.

"No idea. Yet." Asa looked carefully around. He had assumed Daniels and his men had done due diligence on processing the scene, but now he wasn't so sure. He stared at the inexpensive flowered sofa and the rug beneath it.

What had happened? If Tara Brooks had been lured up here by someone, had the killer killed her right away? Violet said she had heard arguing. Had things gotten physical? Doc Adams had not yet filed a report, so Asa could not be sure if any defensive wounds were present.

He sat down on the sofa and looked slowly around, like he

used to do back in the day. He had no idea of what he might find, if anything. Sighing, he got up.

"Kyle, check out the women's bathroom."

"For what?"

"Anything that might not belong."

"In the women's bathroom?"

"I doubt anyone is in there now," Asa reminded him.

"Right." He knocked before going in.

Asa went into the men's bathroom. Two changing stalls, and a toilet and sink behind another door. He looked and found nothing. Discouraged, he went back out.

Back in the baptistry proper, something caught his eye.

At first, he thought it was a piece of fuzz or even a gum wrapper, but it lay just under the sofa. Asa knelt, reached under, and pulled it out.

A woman's pierced-ear earring with a tiny stone that resembled a pearl. It didn't appear to be expensive, and the post was missing.

Kyle came out of the women's bathroom, a touch of red on the young man's face. "Find something?" he asked, seeing Asa on his knees.

"Maybe. Someone dropped an earring."

"Wonder how the cops missed that."

"Indeed," Asa said.

"Could it be...you know...hers?"

"Maybe, but I doubt it. She wasn't wearing earrings," Asa replied. "When was the last baptism we had up here?"

"Three weeks ago."

"Who was here?"

Kyle shrugged. "Just me, the candidate, and the candidate's mom."

“How old was the candidate?”

“Ten.”

“Could it have belonged to the mother?”

“Some girls that age wear them, you know.”

“Call them,” Asa said. “See if anyone’s missing an earring.”

“It could have been here longer than that.”

“You have to start somewhere,” Asa said. “Call them.”

Kyle nodded. “Sure.”

CHAPTER EIGHTEEN

DOC ADAMS SPEAKS

"NO ONE HAS CLAIMED THE EARRING," KYLE said the next morning. "I called every woman who got baptized in the last six months. Checked with Mae and Jackie. Not theirs, either."

"It couldn't have been there that long," Asa said. "If I spotted it, someone else would have before now."

"Could it be an honest clue?"

"Could be, although I'm not sure how yet." Asa leaned back. The phone rang, and he recognized the number. He answered it, spoke for a moment, and hung up.

"That was Doc Adams. He's finished the autopsy on Tara Brooks. Thinks I should get it from him."

"Do you need me to come?"

"Mae says you have a weak stomach when it comes to blood."

"Sort of."

"Stay here. This might not be pleasant."

The doctor met him in the M.E.'s office, located in the

basement of the hospital. Asa had spent many hours in such places, but not since leaving the force, and the familiar smells brought back memories. The office was overtly neat, the desk nearly empty. Adams had his own practice in town and only used this office for examiner business.

"You were right," Adams said. "Strangled. Not enough water in her lungs to drown; she was dead when she went into the pool." He read from the file on his desk. "No drugs in her system, no alcohol. She hadn't had intercourse recently."

"It confirms what I suspected, but doesn't help me much otherwise," Asa said.

Adams put the file down and ran his hands through tousled gray hair. "You taking on this case?"

"I wasn't until they arrested Walter."

"Is the chief okay with it?"

"Sometimes," Asa said. "He wants to solve this, but he's not experienced in homicides."

Adams shrugged. "We haven't had one here in a while. Can't really say."

"Time of death?"

"Between eleven and four. The water makes it a little uncertain."

Asa nodded. "What do you think?"

"Someone knew what they were doing, and were strong enough to do it."

"Like Walter," Asa said. "And someone smaller?"

"Possible. Wouldn't take long."

"What about the belt?"

"It's the one."

"It belongs to Walter."

Adams seemed to take the words in. "Yeah, I was afraid of that."

"Could he have done it?"

"Anything is possible, but I can't see Walter Pence hurting a soul."

"He has means and access to the church. But not a motive."

Adams said, "It seems so random."

"That's what makes it so hard," Asa said.

Asa drove to the church and was back in his office when Kevin Reynolds, Walter's attorney and Mae's son-in-law, came in. "Got a moment?" he asked.

"Sure. Good job getting Walter released."

"Normally I'd be done, but I think not."

"Why?"

"I think they might try to pin this on him again. When they feel they have a strong enough case, they might actually charge him."

"What else could they dredge up?"

Kevin sat down. "Walter had anger issues as a child."

"Anything official?"

"His juvenile records are sealed; I'd have to get a court order to open them up."

"Are you going to do that?"

"If I have to."

"Then how do you know?"

"Mae told me, and I confirmed it. Ted Chambers, the principal of the school where Walter used to go, told me."

"Mind if I talk to him?"

"If you like. Mae has a lot of confidence in your abilities."

"Could his past be a problem?" Asa asked.

Kevin leaned back in his chair. "Maybe. Judge could order the records opened, but it's unlikely they'd do it with Walter so well-known here. But if I were trying the case and I thought there might be something there, I might try to get them unsealed."

"How much of a chance would you have?"

The attorney shrugged. "Depends on the judge, usually. The case against Walter is hanging by a thread, and the chief knows it. That's why he didn't charge him, but he could always change his mind. There's the belt, of course, Walter's access to the church, and the fact that he lives on the property. There is his size, his history with his temper, even his mental faculties."

"A jury could buy it."

Kevin drew in a breath. "Walter's out, and I intend to keep him out. To my knowledge, he's never killed anyone before. Temper, yes; fights too; but that alone doesn't make you a killer. He has no run-ins with the law since his school days and has been a model citizen, held a job." He held up his hands. "The more holes I can put in the case against him, the better the chances he stays a free man."

Asa nodded. "I know, and I appreciate your help. Just keep on top of it."

"Any ideas on the culprit?"

"None so far," Asa remarked.

"But who?" Kevin asked. "Who would kill someone in a church?"

"A place of safety. A holy place."

"Don't forget, Asa, that someone had to have some strength to kill like that."

"And purpose," Asa said. "It's not pretty, killing someone like that. Mae says Walter cries when he sees a wounded bird."

"Maybe when he gets angry, he doesn't cry," Kevin said.

"Doesn't sound like you're helping your client."

"I am," the lawyer answered. "I'm getting ahead of a potential problem."

CHAPTER NINETEEN

SCHOOL DAYS

THEODORE CHAMBERS HAD BEGUN HIS CAreer teaching fifth-grade social studies and history. Twenty years later, he became principal of the high school, and he had retired just a couple of years ago. He was a tall, thin fellow, and Asa found him in overalls and heavy work boots. He met Asa on the front porch of his home, a wooden two-story farmhouse on twenty-five acres just east of town.

"Sorry. I was working on my tractor in the barn," Chambers explained. "Lost track of time." He stuck out a hand and Asa shook it, aware of the calluses and firm grip.

Asa accepted the offer of lemonade, and they sat watching the dozen head of cattle grazing in the field.

"I saw the article on you in the paper," Chambers said. "I remember your wife. Standout student, despite her mother's efforts."

"I'm surprised you remember."

"Some, you never forget," Chambers said.

"Well, I'm hoping you remember one more," Asa said. "Walter Pence."

"Isn't he at your church?"

"He is."

"What do you want to know?"

"I hear Walter had a temper as a kid."

Chambers shook his head. "Walter was a kind kid. We didn't have a lot back then for special-needs kids, and so the teachers and I kinda worked out lesson plans for him. But he was always getting teased by the other kids, and frankly I think that would make anyone mad after a while."

"Anything specific?"

"One kid, Tommy Raines, gave Walter the devil for about a week. I'd spoken to Tommy about it, told him to lay off, but he didn't; and one day on the playground, I was watching from the steps and I noticed Tommy going at him again. At first Walter just stood there and tried to walk away, but Tommy kept on and finally shoved Walter. I started over, intending to stop a fight before it got too far, and something happened."

"What?"

"Walter's expression totally changed. He went from a meek and upset kid to..."

"To what?"

"He picked Tommy up, both hands around Tommy's neck, and lifted the kid off the ground. Tommy was gasping and kicking and flailing about, and it took me and another teacher plus another student to get Walter to let go. He turned and looked at me, and those eyes—those eyes that were normally so kind and caring were dark. They were cold, Pastor. Cold as any I'd ever seen."

"What happened?"

"Walter went over and sat down on one of the swings and began to slowly swing back and forth, oblivious to anyone." Chambers stifled a cough. "It was like the kid blacked out for a while."

"Did he remember it later?"

"I don't know. I heard there was another similar incident before that, but this one was the only one I witnessed."

"Kids were rough on him, huh?"

"You know how cruel kids can be sometimes," Chambers said. "He had some friends too."

"Anyone come to mind?"

"Jeannie Akers. She lives over on Scott Street now."

Asa got up. The lemonade had been delicious. "Thank you so much for your time."

"Do you think Walter killed that girl?"

"I'm trying to show he didn't."

"Good luck," Chambers said. "It would be a shame. I hope you're right."

"Thanks," Asa said. "I hope so too."

"WALTER WAS A SWEETHEART," JEANNIE AKers told Asa. They were sitting in her kitchen while two small children played in the living room. She would occasionally glance through the doorway at them before turning her focus back to him.

"Did he have a lot of friends?"

"Not many, but a few," she said. "Walter had a lot of high energy at times, and he could get a little tiring after a while."

"I hear he had a temper."

"Only when he was pushed. Couple of the jocks used to tease him a lot."

"I hear he lifted Tommy Raines off the ground once."

She thought for a moment. "Wow, I hadn't thought about Tommy in ages. Yeah, Tommy used to pick on Walter, and one day Walter had had enough, I guess."

"Do you know where Tommy is now?"

"Killed in a motorcycle accident in North Carolina three years after graduating."

"Did Walter ever lose it over anything else?"

"Not that I know about. Walter was always sweet and innocent."

"After that incident, I hear that he kind of zoned out."

"Yeah. Took him about a half hour before he was okay."

"What was he like during that time?"

"Just in a daze, a stupor. Unresponsive to anything you asked him. Staring off, as though he saw something that you didn't. Then he came back, and it was like nothing had happened."

"Do you know if he remembered the incident with Tommy?"

"I don't remember," she said. "But no one messed with him much after that." She gestured to the children. "Do you have any kids?"

"A daughter," Asa said. "She's in medical school."

"You must be proud."

"We are."

Jeannie looked at her kids. "Children can be so cruel sometimes."

"You're the second person who has told me that today."

He left Jeannie Akers and was getting in his car when his phone rang.

"Oh, glad to see you have your phone with you. Want to come down to the station?" Daniels asked. "We just nabbed us Tara Brooks's boyfriend."

CHAPTER TWENTY

THE BOYFRIEND

JACK HALL, A.K.A. RED, SAT IN THE STATION'S sole interrogation room. Through the observation window, Asa saw him holding his head in his hands.

Daniels walked in beside Asa. The observation room was a converted utility closet and cramped. "What do you think?"

"You talked to him yet?"

"No. Wanted to wait until you were here."

"That was considerate."

"Maybe you can think of something that I miss." He looked in at Hall, then back to Asa. "You ready?"

Hall raised his head when they walked in, then lowered it again. Daniels sat across the table from him. Asa stood near the door.

"I'm Chief of Police Ned Daniels," the cop began. "You know why you're here?"

"No. I didn't kill Tara," Hall said, face still in his hands.

"Somebody did," Daniels countered. "Look at me, boy, when I'm talking to you."

Hall raised his head. He had thin red hair and a scraggly beard. He'd spent a lot of time in the sun, from the looks of his face and forearms, and his bulk suggested hard manual labor.

"What do you do, Mr. Hall?"

"Construction, when I can get it. Not so much back home right now."

"What brings you here?"

"I told you: I wanted to see her, so I came here."

"How'd you know where she was?"

"She told me."

"Tara told you she was going to come here?"

"She did."

"Did she say why?"

"She said it was an act of atonement," Hall replied. He ran a hand over his face. "She wouldn't tell me what that meant."

"What's the connection between Tara and this town?"

Hall shook his head. "I don't know, Chief. She never would say."

"Why?"

"I asked her. She said it was dangerous if I knew it all, that there were powerful people involved."

"Who?"

Hall let out a sigh. "I wish I knew."

"I think you do, son."

"You're wrong. I don't. I wish I did."

"She have any family?"

"Not really. They pretty much disowned her when she went to prison. Her folks died while she was in the joint. Drug overdose."

"You've been in town how long?"

"I just got here."

"Can you prove that?"

He suddenly straightened as though he had just remembered something. He dug into the pocket of his jeans. "Here."

"What's that?"

"Gas receipt. I filled up at a place an hour before I got here. There's the proof."

Daniels took the receipt and looked at it. "You could have been staying here and drove all the way down to Dalton and filled up."

"I didn't, Chief. I just want to know who killed Tara. I haven't even gotten a bite to eat here. Look, Chief, I drove like blazes to get here, just to find out she's dead; so I came to the cops because I wanted to know what had happened. That's all."

"She's been here a while now. Why did you wait so long?"

"I had a job building a house and couldn't leave. I needed the money."

"Did you two get along?"

"Sure."

"You two ever fight?"

"Sure. Doesn't everyone?"

"You ever get violent with her?"

Hall pointed a finger. "Listen, cop, don't think I don't know what you're doing. I didn't kill Tara; I wasn't even in town when it happened. So don't try your stupid games with me. I know the tricks."

"I'm sure you do." Daniels pulled out a sheet of paper. "I took the liberty of doing some research. You're no stranger to the legal system, Mr. Hall. Let's see...burglary, drug possession—"

"It was just pot," Hall said. "Nothing more."

"—here's another burglary, oooh, possession of burglary tools, assault; hmm, that's interesting..." Daniels laid the paper down. He spun the folder around so that the dead face of Tara Brooks showed. "If I go out there and search your vehicle, Mr. Hall, am I going to get any surprises?"

"I've been clean for three years," he said. "Search away."

"You sure?"

"I'm done talking," he said. "Lock me up, in which case I want a lawyer. Otherwise let me go. I want to see Tara."

Daniels put the evidence bag containing the bracelet found at Walter's place on the table in front of Hall. "You recognize this?"

"Never seen it before."

"What do you mean?"

"I've never seen it before," Hall insisted.

"Isn't that Tara's?"

Hall chuckled. "Tara wouldn't be caught dead with that cheap thing. She only wore expensive bracelets."

"Did she wear one all the time?"

"Ever since she left the halfway house."

"And you're positive it's not hers?"

"Chief, I know—knew that girl. And dating her trained me to spot cheap jewelry. That's not Tara's."

Daniels glanced at Asa, then pointed at Hall. He shoved a white legal pad in front of Hall. "Write down where you were, beginning when you left Kentucky, until you came here. Then sign it."

Hall picked up the offered pen and began to write.

Daniels walked out of the room, and Asa joined him. "What do you think?" Daniels asked.

"Question is, what do you think?"

"Think he's lying about the bracelet?"

"I don't think so," Asa said.

A puzzled expression came onto Daniels's face. "Why not?"

"Why would he lie? It doesn't incriminate him to admit it, if it was hers. Besides, I think there's something else at play in this mystery."

"Like what?"

"Not sure yet."

"Well," Daniels said. "We're going to search his truck, see what we can find."

Hall drove a late-model pickup. The search didn't take long.

"Nothing of interest," Daniels said, dejection in his tone. "No drugs, no paraphernalia."

Asa merely grunted and leaned against the fender.

"Something on your mind?" Daniels asked.

Asa shook his head. "I hate it when I can't make the pieces fit."

"I don't feel so stupid, then," Daniels said. "Hall wants to go see Tara at the morgue. I guess I'll drive him down."

"If he doesn't mind, Chief," Asa looked up, "I'd like to do it."

"You sure?"

"Yeah."

They went back inside. Hall came out into the lobby with the notepad. "Here."

Daniels put it on the counter and looked at it. "You forgot to sign it."

Hall took the pen and scribbled an illegible signature at the bottom. "Satisfied?"

"Immensely," Daniels retorted.

Asa glanced back behind the partition to see Carla Reed at her desk. He walked over.

"I heard you did some digging on Tara," he said.

She nodded. "The boyfriend was right. The few relatives she has left don't really want to keep in touch with her."

"It happens sometimes," Asa said. For the first time, he noticed the circular mirror on the wall. It allowed the office people a view of the front counter, while the officers could keep out of view of the public. Ingenious, Asa thought.

Hall was being released and heading to the door. Now came the hard part.

CHAPTER TWENTY-ONE

ASA AND RED TAKE A RIDE

"WHO ARE YOU?" HALL ASKED WHEN HE got into Asa's car.

Asa introduced himself. "I'm the pastor of the church where Tara was found."

"I didn't know she was killed in a church."

"I'm afraid so," Asa said. "And I thought since many find this an unpleasant experience, I might be of some help."

"You're not gonna try to get me saved, are you, Reverend?"

"God does the saving; I just arrange the meeting," Asa said. "Besides, I wanted to talk with you for a minute away from Chief Daniels."

"I told him there was nothing in the truck."

"Yes, you did. How long had you and Tara been dating?"

"Not long. Right after she got out of the halfway house."

"When was that?"

"About six months ago."

"Did she ever talk about the incident that sent her to jail?"

"DUI. She hit and killed some poor bast—dude—one night."

"And she claimed she didn't do it."

"Yes."

"Who did do it?"

"Her best friend, she said. CC. They'd been best friends since first grade."

"CC got a name?"

Hall shook his head. "Never would say. Just CC."

"So according to Tara, CC had been driving the car?"

"Supposedly. They were both drinking, but CC had been driving. When the accident happened, CC ran off, and her dad was well known in town and pretty much got her off the hook. Cops didn't even question her, I don't think."

"And you weren't around then?"

Hall shook his head. "No, I grew up across the line in Tennessee."

"So Tara took the fall," Asa said. "That would make a person angry."

"She was, too."

"Do you know where CC might be?"

"No idea," Hall answered. "She didn't look it, Reverend, but Tara was smart. She understood finance, stocks. One night she starts talking to me about black holes and stuff. She read a lot, too."

"What about her family?"

"Her parents are dead. Both of them, caught up in painkillers. It's pretty bad in Kentucky—the whole area."

"Any other kin that you know about?"

"After she went to prison, her folks died, and her other relatives pretty much wrote her off or she didn't want them around. She didn't say why." He looked out the window. "I didn't know much about her, really."

"How can you date someone and not know that much about them?"

"Look, we both have—had—scars, and we just wanted to forget that part and move forward. Didn't seem like much, but we were slowly getting to know each other. Peel away the layers one at a time, if you like."

"Sounds like she might have had some other secrets."

"Look, Rev, you might not believe me, but I believe in the Almighty, and I know I'll have to answer for my life one day. God knows, I have plenty to answer for. But I swear I didn't kill her."

"I know," Asa said.

"That cop doesn't think so."

"He'll come around," Asa said. He pulled into the parking lot. "We're here."

Doctor Adams met them beside a curtain that Asa knew covered a window.

"Are you ready?" Asa asked Red.

Hall merely nodded, and Doc pulled the curtain aside to reveal Tara Brooks on a gurney with just her head exposed. Hall put a fist to his mouth and nodded again; Doc drew the curtain closed.

"Do you want to sit down?" Asa asked him.

Hall shook his head. "Do they have any suspects?"

"Nothing concrete," Asa said. "They're working on it, I promise."

"If I find him—" Hall said. "If I find out who killed my Tara, I'm going to kill them."

"No," Asa shook his head. "That is not what you do—"

"—and if they sit on this case and don't do anything, they will rue the day." He turned away. "Meet you in the car, Rev."

Asa blew out some air. Adams nodded at Hall's receding frame. "He's wound pretty tight, Pastor. Better be on your guard."

"I know," Asa said. "Thanks, Doc."

Hall was standing by the car, arms folded across his chest and smoking a cigarette.

"For what it's worth, I'm sorry," Asa said.

"Want one?" Hall held up the pack.

"Quit smoking in college," Asa said.

"I figured. Preachers don't smoke, drink, anything like that."

"You might be surprised," Asa said. "One of the great preachers of the faith loved a good cigar in his day. Come on, I'll take you back to your truck."

"I don't have a lot of faith in the police here," Hall said.

"I understand, but I assure you the killer will be found."

"I don't share your optimism, Reverend." Hall looked out the window. "They better hope I don't find them first."

"Don't do something stupid," Asa said.

"Wouldn't be the first time."

"And you'd end up in prison instead of them. Not a smart move."

Finally, Hall glanced over at the preacher. "You're not like a lot of the preachers I've met."

"How so?"

"You haven't spoken to me at all about getting saved or repenting."

"I don't think it's the time or place," Asa said. "Do you want me to?"

"She's just...dead. Lying there like that." Hall began to shake his head. "This can't stand, Reverend."

"It won't. Justice will be served, Mr. Hall, I promise you that."

They pulled into the station, and Hall got out.

"Mr. Hall?"

"Yeah?"

"Remember what I said. Don't do anything stupid," Asa said.

Hall looked at Asa and stormed off toward his truck.

CHAPTER TWENTY-TWO

THREE MEETINGS

NED DANIELS TOOK A DEEP BREATH BEFORE stepping into the mayor's office. Foster sat behind the large cluttered desk and, as soon as the chief entered, jerked a thumb toward the window that overlooked Main Street.

"Eight years," he said. "Eight years without a murder in this town, and you haven't charged anyone yet. What about Pence?"

"The evidence was spotty, sir," Daniels said. "And arresting is not the same as charging."

"Tell that to that pastor," Foster responded. "He's probably jumping through hoops to keep his boy out of jail. May scurry him off somewhere."

"No, sir."

"What do you mean, 'no, sir'?"

"Reverend Carter wouldn't do that. If Pence is guilty, he won't hinder the findings."

"Need I remind you that elections are coming up? Your job and mine are on the line, Ned. And we got a murder. We've got a pastor who's going around town, talking to people, questioning them, acting like he's Sherlock Holmes or something. Meanwhile, my Chief of Police and his band of merry men sit on their tails and do nothing." Foster leaned forward and pointed a finger at Daniels. "I want this case solved, Chief."

"It's not that simple."

"It *is* that simple. Walter Pence killed that girl, end of story."

Daniels got up. "Uh-huh." He walked out, and Foster watched him go. Alone in his office, the mayor leaned back and composed himself.

KAY RALTON LEFT THE GREETING-CARD SHOP and turned toward Market. She was in front of the flower shop when she nearly ran into someone. She looked up and saw the face of Pat Cobb. He blocked her path.

"Pat, what are you—?"

"What did you tell the cops, Kay?"

"What are you talking about? Get out of the way!"

"Listen. I'm not getting dragged into this thing. You'd better keep your mouth shut about me and Tara, see? Blabbermouths can find themselves in deep trouble."

"What are you talking about?"

"You just remember what I said." Cobb pointed at her. "I'm not going back to jail for no one." He stormed past her, and she watched him go for a long moment. She looked into the flower shop. Violet Corbin stared back at her.

ASA SAT BACK IN HIS CHAIR WITH A SIGH AND glanced at his watch. It was late; time had gotten away from him and it was already dark outside. Ellen would have supper waiting for him, but he'd have to warm it up.

The church was quiet, and Asa put away the sermon notes he'd prepared and locked up the office. Tara's face kept appearing in his head.

Lord, if you want me to solve this, you're going to have to give me wisdom.

He walked into the parking lot. A bicycle was leaning against one of the large oaks that adorned the complex. Asa stood for a long moment, staring at it. Something tried to shake itself loose in his brain.

"Evening, Pastor."

Violet Corbin approached the bike.

Asa smiled. "Evening. Violet, isn't it?"

"That's right." She avoided his gaze for the most part; when she did look at him, she focused on his chest or shoes.

"Can't sleep?"

"I sleep better after a good stroll and bike ride."

"Do you always do it here, in the parking lot?"

She gave a small nod. "It's quiet here at night. Calm."

A slight breeze wafted toward him, and he caught the faint whiff of perfume. "I like your perfume. I think my wife wears that."

She flushed. "Ooh, yeah. A friend gave that to me."

"You have nice friends."

She smiled, a slight coy smile. "Yeah, I do."

A screech of tires caused him to turn. Headlights filled his vision, and the vehicle was nearly on him. Asa grabbed Violet and dove on top of her onto the grass near the oak tree, narrowly avoiding the vehicle's right fender. The vehicle continued onward and banged into the brick wall of a flower bed. It backed up and raced away, but not before Asa saw it—a truck—more clearly in the parking-lot lights. Beneath him, Violet shivered, and a soft sob escaped her. Asa got to his feet and pulled Violet up with him. "Are you okay?"

She stood on shaky legs and glanced up at Asa. She was scared to death.

"Come on," Asa said. "Let's get you inside."

Ellen was her usual gracious self, giving Violet tea and motherly pats on the shoulder. Violet had calmed down some and declined Asa's offer to drive her home, insisting that she wanted to ride her bike. She bid them a meek good evening, thanked them both, and left.

Ellen put the cups and saucers into the dishwasher.

"A rather peculiar woman."

"Yeah."

"She seems to visit the church a lot," Ellen said.

"She says she likes to walk there. She finds it quiet."

"Still..." Ellen turned. "Are you okay?"

"I'm fine."

The doorbell rang, and Daniels joined them in the kitchen. He refused Ellen's offer of food or coffee, saying he'd never sleep if he had a cup this late. The chief was off duty, wearing jeans and a polo shirt with the department logo on the chest. A badge hung on his belt, and he wore his sidearm in a holster on his right hip.

"And you're sure it was Hall's truck?"

"Yeah, I'm sure," Asa said between bites. "And he hit the flower-bed wall near the entrance on his way out. Had to have made a dent or two in the fender."

"And you were nice to him," Daniels said. "That boy..." He sighed. "I'll swing by his motel, see if he's there. If so, I'll bust him."

"Mind if I tag along?"

"You got a gun?"

"That's what *you're* for," Asa answered.

They stopped in the motel office and learned that Hall was staying in room 5. His truck was in a slot in front, and Asa pointed to the dent in the left fender. Daniels nodded, and they approached the door.

"You'd best step back, Reverend."

Asa found himself standing beside the door and realized his training hadn't left him, even after all these years. How many home and apartment doors had he knocked on, standing off to the side in case someone shot through the door? Daniels was ready to knock when Asa stopped him and reached over, rapped on the door.

"Mr. Hall? It's Reverend Carter. I'd like to talk for a moment."

They paused and waited. There was no sound from inside.

Again, Asa knocked. "Mr. Hall?" He glanced at Daniels, who held up the passkey. Asa unlocked it and gave the nod. Daniels charged in, gun out.

"Oh, geez..." Daniels said.

Asa saw the problem. Red Hall sat on the floor, leaning back against the bed. His head was slumped to one side, tongue slightly out. A needle remained in Hall's right arm.

Daniels put two fingers on the neck, then looked at Asa and shook his head. Hall was very dead.

CHAPTER TWENTY-THREE

ANOTHER BODY

"WELL..." DANIELS SAID. "SH–SHOOT."

By now, they'd called everyone they needed to, and Carla Reed had been the first to arrive. She was wearing jeans instead of the usual slacks, and a short-sleeve blouse, but she went to work. Moments later, two more officers showed up and began to work the scene.

"Looks like an overdose," Daniels said. A nearly empty scotch bottle was on the nightstand. "He was on a bender."

"That's a lot of booze, that's for sure," Asa agreed.

"He didn't have anything in his truck," Reed said. "Must have had his stash here."

"Looks like the halfway house didn't work," Daniels said. He turned to Asa. "What am I missing?"

"Have them talk to the staff, guests, see if anyone heard or saw anything," Asa said.

"Why?"

"Cover your bases, Chief. Sometimes you only get one shot.

Never assume."

"Right." Daniels turned to a young officer near the door. "Go and talk to the staff and guests. See if they heard or saw anything."

"Right, Chief."

Asa walked out of the room as another officer began photographing the scene. He leaned against the worn brick exterior and sighed.

Daniels walked over to him. "Something wrong, Pastor?"

"I don't know," Asa said. "Something I'm missing." He shook his head. "Too long off the job, Chief."

"Look, he's a known addict, just out of rehab. He comes here, sees his girl dead on a slab, and starts drinking. That much booze with a shot of—well, whatever he took—and it was enough to kill him. Probably enough to kill an elephant. He was wasted when he tried to run you over."

The chief was right, Asa had to admit. There was no note, so suicide seemed possible but unlikely.

Doc Adams arrived. He strode, businesslike, into the room. Asa and Daniels followed. They stood silently while Adams examined what was left of Red Hall.

"Looks like an OD, or at least alcohol poisoning or both," Adams said. "Won't know for sure until I get him on the table."

"How long?" Asa asked.

"How long to get him on the table?"

"No, Doc, how long has he been dead?"

Adams checked the face and arms. "Slight rigor in the arms. I'd say no more than three hours." The doc looked around. "What did he inject?"

"No sign of anything, Doc," Asa said. He took out his handkerchief and picked up the hypodermic, looked at it closely. "Be sure you bag this, Chief."

"Sure. Anything of note?"

"Don't know," Asa said. The admission bothered him.

CARLA REED DROVE HIM HOME.

"What do you think?" she asked.

"It's a darn shame," Asa said. "Maybe I should have done more."

"What could you have done?"

"I don't know. But it bothers me. He was pretty upset when I left him. Understandable, I guess, but maybe I should have talked more with him."

"Look, Hall was a troubled guy. He may have gotten clean but he relapsed. By the way, we found a small amount of heroin in his suitcase. That's probably what he used." Reed shook her head. "There was little you could have done."

Asa forced his thoughts away from the dead man. He pointed to Carla Reed's right forearm. "That's quite a scar."

The faded white scar ran down her forearm. She grinned. "When I was seven. Romping in the kitchen and did a Spider-Man leap right through our sliding glass door. Quick thinking on my mom's part kept me from bleeding to death."

They drove in silence for a moment before Reed said, "Can I ask you something?"

"Of course."

"Why'd you quit being a cop?"

"To be honest, I felt the call to go into the ministry."

"What does that feel like?"

He shrugged. "Hard to pinpoint, really. It wasn't an overnight decision. You pray about it, try to listen, and see if God speaks."

"And does He?"

"Sometimes. A lot of times He gives you signs. I had plenty of them that kept drawing me toward it. So, I did."

"Any regrets?"

"None."

"And now you're back to doing it again."

"I just want to find out who killed this girl. And I will."

"You don't think Walter did it?"

"Of course not."

"Then who did?"

"I don't know. But I'm going to find out."

They pulled up to Asa's house. "Thanks for the ride, Officer Reed."

"Welcome." She drove off. Asa walked into the house. As usual, Ellen was sitting at the kitchen table, grading papers.

"Aren't you up late?"

"What happened?"

"Dead. OD from the looks of it," Asa said. He sat on the sofa with a sigh and took off his shoes.

Ellen put her red pen down. "What's wrong?"

"Nothing."

She gave him the look that said she knew him too well not to notice. "You don't say that like you mean it."

"I can't think of a reason to doubt it," he said. "But maybe..." He let the thought trail off.

"You're missing something," she said. "You'll figure it out."

"I wish I had your confidence."

"Asa, you haven't done this in two decades. Only right that you're not at the apex of your game. It will happen."

"I need to be if I'm going to find the killer."

She bent down and kissed him. "Go to bed. We have the seniors fellowship dinner tomorrow."

"I don't consider myself to be a senior. Yet."

"Even so, you have to go. The pastor needs to be there."

"Oh, bring *that* argument into it," he said.

CHAPTER TWENTY-FOUR

AN ODD THING

Chief Daniels let out a sigh and smiled, leaning back in his chair. He hadn't admitted it to anyone, but he wasn't sure about any of this at the moment. He also didn't like being railroaded and manipulated, and the fact that the mayor was trying to push him into something made Daniels feel as though he needed to rethink things. Pence had seemed the perfect suspect, but Asa was right: He had evidence, but nothing that linked Walter directly to the crime.

But Hall…now, that was a different story. A dead guy, drug history, had a relationship with the deceased. It was an early Christmas present, wrapped up and tied with a neat little bow.

Asa sat in front of him. The pastor, Daniels had discovered, had been a top detective on the Chicago PD. He had found several articles from Chicago papers about Detective First Grade Asa Carter solving this murder or that. Maybe he was right, Daniels mused. Maybe he needed to rethink Pence's guilt.

"Well, Rev, I guess that disproves your theory. Jack Hall comes into town, lures her—or drives her to the lot. He picks the lock on the door, takes her to the baptistry, and strangles her."

"The time stamp on the receipt, Chief."

"You and I both know he could have pulled that off. He could have easily gotten gas there after he killed her, when we were all running around chasing our tails, then come back into town like he'd just arrived once she'd been identified."

"Why in the world would he have come back? He comes into town, kills Tara, drives to Dalton and gets gas, then comes back?"

"To throw suspicion off of him," Daniels said.

"How could he have been a suspect in the first place, Chief, when no one knew he was even here? No one ever heard of Red Hall until he showed up in your station. If he killed Tara, he could have just left and gotten away clean."

Daniels slumped.

"Look, Rev, if he's capable of killing her, that tells me he's probably assaulted her before. Maybe she came here to escape him. To try to start over."

"Maybe, but it doesn't explain his actions. Red Hall didn't kill her; if he did and had the nerve to come back to try to throw suspicion off of himself, then he was an idiot."

"Maybe he *was* an idiot," Daniels said.

"How would Red Hall get Walter's belt?"

"Oh, Asa, you know that kid is addlebrained. He probably left it there. Mae tells me he does his laundry there. I bet he left it lying there—maybe forgot about it. Hall sees it and decides it's the perfect murder weapon."

"Did you check it for prints?"

"Of course. Nothing back from the lab yet."

"So, I can't prove Hall didn't kill her," Asa said.

"Unless you come across something else that knocks it off the table," Daniels said. He sipped his coffee. "But if someone else ends up dead, I might give you a call. You nailed it on the head with the cause of death for her."

"Thanks, but maybe I'll stick to God," Asa said. "Thanks for the coffee."

Asa left the police station and walked the three blocks to the Red Oak Diner, where he ordered a club sandwich. The coffee weighed heavy on him, so he surprised the waitress by ordering milk. A figure caught his gaze, and he looked to see Father Herbert Quinn looking down at him. Quinn was a chunky fellow with a round face and small round frameless glasses that always seemed too small for his face. He caught the waitress's attention and ordered a tuna sandwich and sweet tea. He plopped down across from Asa with a sigh.

"You look like a troubled soul," Quinn said.

"Hungry is more like it," Asa retorted.

"Now, *that* we have in common," Quinn said. He asked how Ellen was settling into the parsonage, if Asa had finished work on his first sermon yet, and what his thoughts were on Glen Pines. Asa humored him, waiting until Quinn worked his way around to what he really wanted to talk about. "I heard they caught the murderer."

Asa shrugged. "He's dead, so we will never know."

"But he did kill her?"

Another shrug. "Chief Daniels seems to think so."

"You, however..." Quinn started and paused while the waitress brought his lunch. He blessed his food and shook a generous dose of pepper over the tuna before replacing the top slice of wheat bread. "You don't look convinced."

"I'm not. At least not completely."

"And why not?"

"Because Hall was right-handed and the needle was in his right arm. Plus, there was no sign of any drug paraphernalia in the room. If Hall was using, there should be some evidence of it."

"Could you be...mistaken?"

"That's what I'm trying to figure out, Herb, I really am. By the way, I forgot to thank you for your nice introduction to the regional clergy meeting. I was humbled by the invite."

"You're a part of our little brotherhood now," Quinn said. "I was worried that it was too soon, you barely getting settled and all."

"And then the murders."

"*Especially* the murders." Quinn leaned in. "Asa, have you prayed about your concerns on the solution the police have come up with?"

"I am doing so."

"And any news?"

"Not yet, I'm afraid," Asa said. "Although these things are usually never in our time, but His."

"True," Quinn agreed. "I must admit, it does seem odd that Hall would choose a church."

"He didn't strike me as much of a churchgoer," Asa said.

Quinn nodded. "Odd. Well, I will pray for the truth to come out. I'm afraid that is all I can do for now."

"I appreciate it."

"If I may, I wanted to talk to you about something else."

"Fire away."

"Ran into Doc Adams. Said no one has claimed Tara Brooks's body. We talked about a funeral for her."

"You're right. We need to lay her to rest."

"I thought maybe a simple graveside service. My church will go in half on a plot for her."

"Go the other half and we'll cover the casket."

"Then you'll have the worst end of the deal."

"I owe her that much. She was killed on holy ground. My church."

"You owe her nothing, Asa," Quinn said.

"I owe her closure, Herb. I owe her to find the killer and see that justice is served." He spotted someone on the sidewalk. "Excuse me a minute."

He walked outside to find Pat Cobb smoking a cigarette and leaning against a light pole.

"Mr. Cobb."

Cobb turned and almost took a step back. "That hurt when you hit me with the car door."

"Shouldn't have been running from the cops."

"Pretty gutsy for a preacher."

"Maybe," Asa said. "You're out on bail, I take it."

"What's it to you?"

"You have a problem, Mr. Cobb, whether you realize it or not. You were seen talking to the victim, and you threatened her. You have a criminal record, including burglary. You are known to have a temper, and you are certainly strong enough to have strangled her."

"I didn't kill her."

"When was the last time you talked to Tara?"

"You know that."

"The day you threatened her?"

"I told you, I was angry and half in the bag."

"Nevertheless, threatening to kill someone can be viewed as a serious crime in most states," Asa said. "Anyone else interested in Tara or have a problem with her?"

"Why ask me?"

"Because you were interested in her and my guess is that if she had anyone else around vying for her attention, you'd know about it."

"You think you know me?"

"I've known dozens like you," Asa said. "Well? Anyone else here interested in Tara?"

"No one that I know of," Hall answered. "She told me she had a boyfriend back home, and that was that."

"And that was the last time you spoke to her?"

"Yes."

"Was it the last time you saw her?"

Hall hesitated. "Well, no. I saw her when she left work that night. I was over there—" he pointed to a bench in front of a shoe store.

"What were you doing there?"

"Waiting for her to leave."

"Why?"

He shrugged. "Don't know. I was trying to see if she'd talk to me."

"And she didn't?"

"No. She didn't even notice me."

"Anything unusual about her?"

"She looked nervous. Even scared."

"And you didn't talk to her."

Cobb shook his head. "No. I was going to, but I changed my mind."

"Tara was killed in my church. The killer picked the lock on the door to get in."

"So..."

Asa stared at him. "What do you think?"

"You think I can pick a lock?"

"With your history of burglary, I'd bet on it. Most good burglars can."

Something flickered across Cobb's face. "So, you think I did it?"

Asa said "The church door that was picked. Single-cylinder dead-bolt lock on it. Easy?"

Cobb paused for a moment. "I wouldn't know."

"Oh, come on."

"You gonna tell the chief?"

"Did you break into my church and kill Tara Brooks?"

"No."

"Then this is between us," Asa said. "Again, a single-cylinder dead bolt."

"Easy *peasey*, Reverend," Cobb said. "Most new lock pickers practice on those."

"Okay. Thank you." Asa walked back into the diner. He felt Cobb's gaze on his back, but he went in and sat.

Quinn looked through the window at Cobb, then back at Asa. "What was that all about?"

"Talking to a gentleman who confirmed a suspicion of mine."

"You're a pastor, not a cop."

"Maybe not," Asa said. "But I'm going to find who did this."

CHAPTER TWENTY-FIVE

THE LUNCHEON

IT WAS IN THE FIRST FIVE MINUTES OF THE DINNER that Asa realized that he had not known how many seniors occupied the pews at Grace Gospel Church. Judging by the attendance, there were quite a few. The food consisted of lunch-meat sandwiches cut into triangles, veggie trays, and desserts made by one of the Sunday school classes. There was tea, sweet and unsweet, and coffee. Asa sat beside his wife and ate while, across the table, Dorothy Prader made a show of not trying to call attention to her new pearl necklace by touching it every ten seconds.

"That was a nice sermon you gave, Pastor, yes, sir. Very nice. I was so inspired."

"Thank you. I appreciate that."

Dorothy's white hair was immaculately coiffed, and her nails appeared to have been done that morning. She adjusted her glasses, and then her smile turned upside down.

"Imagine the shock of finding that poor young woman dead on your first day here. How awful that must have been."

"Indeed," Asa said. "You didn't by chance know her, did you?"

"Heavens, no. Why would I?"

"Well, she worked at the diner, so I thought you might have talked to her or something."

"Well, she was probably up to no good, I can bet you," she said. "Those tattoos and hair...something was amiss, let me tell you."

"Don't you live right across the street, Miss Prader?"

"For the last thirty years," she said with pride. "Never have to drive to church, let me tell you."

"Did you notice anything the night of the murder?"

The woman gave Asa a quizzical look. "What time was she killed?"

"Around midnight."

"Oh, no, I was asleep. Don't begin to stir until about six. I sleep like a log, in spite of the fact that my husband—Gregory was his name—passed on. I thought I'd have trouble sleeping after he went on to glory, but I sleep better than I have in years." Her brow furrowed. "Wonder what that means."

Asa smiled and grabbed his paper plate. "Excuse me."

He got up and found that Ellen had abandoned him for the dessert line.

"How's Dorothy Prader?"

"I take it you remember her?"

Ellen smiled. "Her husband owned a hardware store when I was a kid. Sold it to someone when he retired and it didn't stay open long. Some said he died of a broken heart over that."

"What about her?"

"He left her well off, and she's not afraid of showing it."

Asa nodded. "She was asleep the night of the murder." He

chose a piece of apple pie with a latticework crust that he knew tasted as sinful as it looked even before he added whipped cream. He was savoring the flavor when several other seniors came over to him, introducing themselves and commenting on how pleased they were to have him.

"It was such a shock," Gladys Gilmore said. "To have our beloved shepherd take off with that...floozy."

"Gladys," a tall man with a white moustache chided.

"Well, she was," Gladys said. "Seducing a man of God like that. It's inexcusable, Roy, and you know it."

"Nobody seduced him into stealing from the treasury," Roy said.

"That was her doing, I bet," Gladys said. "Talked him into it."

Roy said nothing; merely looked at Asa and shook his head. "Any news on the dead girl, Pastor?"

"Not much, I'm afraid."

"I heard there's been another murder. The girl's boyfriend."

"I'm afraid I can't tell you much about that," Asa said.

Gladys lowered her voice. "You don't believe that—Walter did it?"

Roy rolled his eyes. "Gladys, for heaven's sake. Of course he didn't."

"Well, it's important to know for sure in these things," she insisted. "I watch the mystery channel on TV, after all. I know these things." Gladys turned her attention back to Asa. "What do you think?"

"I don't think Walter did it," Asa said.

"Well, the police are surely proving their incompetence," Gladys went on. "That lawyer fella on TV would have had it solved in an hour." She strode off, and Roy watched her go. He shook his head again.

"I don't know, Pastor. Sometimes I don't think her bread's quite done."

Asa couldn't argue with that.

Roy leaned closer. "Listen, we're all pretty rattled about what happened. First with the pastor, and now with the murders. Some people say it's the devil at work."

"Well, he is a big proponent of lust, greed, and murder," Asa said.

After mingling for what he deemed to be an appropriate amount of time, he joined Ellen, who was in deep conversation with an elderly man who leaned on a cane and put one hand on Ellen's shoulder.

"Asa, I'd like you to meet Bobby Roman, my high school math teacher."

"A pleasure," Asa said.

"Likewise. Your wife was a standout student. I knew she'd do well." Roman was nearing ninety, he said, and he was bent and slow, but his mind seemed clear.

"She credits you for her love of it," Asa said.

Roman shrugged off the compliment. "She's being too kind."

Ellen walked away to speak to someone, and the old man leaned closer to Asa. "Two murders in this town in such a short amount of time. It's unbelievable."

"It's tragic," Asa said.

Roman nodded in agreement. "We're all praying for you."

"I appreciate it," Asa said. *God knows, I need all the help I can get.*

CHAPTER TWENTY-SIX

THE DEBT AND A MEETING

THE MAYOR'S SECRETARY WAS A MIDDLE-AGED woman named Janice with platinum blond hair and a pleasant demeanor so syrupy sweet that it could border on eerie. She motioned Carla Reed in. "He'll see you now, Officer."

"Thanks."

Carla paused for a heartbeat at the door. She closed her eyes for a long moment before walking in.

Ron Foster stood at the window that offered him a third-story view of the town. The mayor was dressed in slacks and a long-sleeved dress shirt, open at the collar, the sleeves rolled half-way up his forearms.

"Nice of you to come."

"Mr. Mayor," Reed said.

"Oh, we're being formal, are we, Carla?"

"What do you want?" she asked.

"Some answers."

"To?"

"This whole thing has gotten completely out of hand. Two people dead, and your boss is looking more like Barney Fife. Now he tells me Hall didn't kill the girl?"

"I know."

"You know. Well, that's a relief."

"Mr. Mayor, let me just talk to him."

"And there's this preacher fellow..."

"He used to be a homicide detective back in Chicago," Reed said. "He's the one that's talking the chief out of Hall's guilt."

"And this Pence fellow, too, from what I hear."

"The evidence we have—" Reed began "—probably won't be enough to convict. And he has a good attorney, well..."

"You need to fix this," Foster said. "You need to do what you have to do."

"Look, I'm just a patrol officer."

"I can't have two unsolved murders in this town," Foster said. "There are other...considerations."

"Ron, I don't think—"

"Let me tell you what to think, Carla. Remember this: I own you. Your job, your reputation, your orbit around the universe—all of it—is in my hands."

Her jaw tightened, and she closed her eyes and bit her lip.

"Do you understand that, or have you forgotten your debt to me?"

"I haven't. You know how grateful I am."

"Then you have that chance again to express your gratitude. Tonight, at nine. Same place."

"Wife out of town?"

"None of your concern. Be there."

"I have work in the morning."

"Nine," he said. He walked to her, put his hand on the back of her head, drew her to him, and kissed her hard on the mouth. She started to protest, but stopped herself. He released her, and she glared at him. "You're a bastard."

He smiled. "Don't be late."

She stormed out, closing the door behind her. Ron watched her go and thought for a moment. He went to his desk and buzzed his secretary.

"Janice, get me the good Reverend Carter at Grace Gospel Church. I would like a chat with him."

ASA HAD NEVER MET THE MAYOR, BUT HE knew what Foster looked like. His face was usually in the small newspaper published every week, so Asa spotted him easily. Mayor Foster sat in a corner booth, the remnants of a large salad and a diet soda in front of him.

"Good morning, Mr. Mayor. I'm Reverend Asa Carter."

The mayor looked up from his paper. "Ah, yes, Reverend. So glad to meet you at last. Have a seat, please."

"Thank you." Asa sat.

"Something to eat?" Foster did a quick assessment. He had found himself to be pretty good at reading people. This reverend seemed calm, peaceful, and even warm. But there was something in the eyes that unnerved the mayor a little. There was a bright, inquisitive mind behind those glasses and the kind smile. But there was also, Foster sensed, a fierce tenacity. Like a dog with a bone, Asa Carter would not let go of things easily.

Asa held up a palm. "Oh, no, thanks. My wife fed me already."

"She is a teacher at the high school, I understand."

"Yes."

"How is she enjoying it?"

"She loves it."

"Glad to hear it. Look, Reverend, I need a little favor," the mayor said. "We have a nice little town here in Glen Pines, wouldn't you agree?"

"I would."

Foster nodded in the way politicians do when you agree with them. "Now, you show up, and suddenly we've had two rather tragic deaths, and people are upset and anxious. They'd like these things solved. I personally appointed Ned Daniels to be chief, and he's a good cop. He says he's solved the case, and, as far as I'm concerned, that's that."

Asa didn't respond. He merely looked at the mayor, fingertips touching in that way he had when he was analyzing a situation. *Wait long enough and he'll start talking again*, he thought. *People like him can't help themselves.*

"I know you used to be a cop. But you're not anymore."

"I'm aware of that."

"So how about you stick to saving souls and let Daniels worry about murders? The last thing we need here is to keep dredging up this unpleasantness for everyone."

"But what about justice? Surely you must be in favor of justice?"

"Oh, of course, Reverend. But nothing more can be gained by rehashing all this."

"Don't forget, sir, the woman was killed in my church."

"I am aware of that. A tragic thing piled on top of all the other stuff your congregation has had to face in the last six months. Best to let it go and let people breathe again. After all, your janitor stands a good chance of being the prime suspect and all. Took some muscle to strangle a person like that. And I'm not one for advocating the prosecution of a man with...well, special needs; but, as I see it, we close this case and your boy can continue doing his thing, provided he behaves himself."

"Walter didn't kill that girl, Mr. Mayor."

Foster made a seesaw motion with a palm. "Maybe. Maybe not."

Asa smiled his best smile and stood. "Well, thanks for the advice, Mr. Mayor. I'm glad we had this talk and finally got to meet. You're invited to Sunday services anytime you want. We'd be pleased to have you."

Foster shook his hand. "Pleasure as well. Good day, Reverend."

"Oh, by the way," Asa turned. "How did you know she was strangled? That wasn't released to the papers."

For a second, something flickered across Foster's eyes. "I believe the chief told me."

"I don't think even the chief is quite that sloppy."

"What are you suggesting, Reverend?"

Asa walked away, knowing that the mayor was eyeing him as he left. He sniffed. The mayor's cologne smelled familiar.

CHAPTER TWENTY-SEVEN

ASA ISN'T CONVINCED

KYLE WALKED INTO ASA'S OFFICE. THE YOUNG minister's face held a touch of disappointment. "I was talking to Mae. She said the case had been solved."

"What's wrong with that?" Asa asked.

"I was hoping the murder would be solved like in the movies. You know, a car chase, bullets flying."

"They rarely end like that," Asa said.

Kyle plopped down on the sofa. "Still…it would have been exciting."

"Not really."

"You don't find car chases exciting?"

Asa glanced up from his work. "Nor bullets flying."

Kyle sighed.

"There is one glimmer of hope for you, as far as I can see," Asa said.

"What's that?"

"I'm not convinced Jack Hall killed her."

"Chief Daniels seems convinced."

Asa snorted. "Chief Daniels is under pressure from the mayor to wrap this up. Jack Hall's death gives him a nice solution wrapped in a red ribbon."

"And it would clear Walter."

"Yes."

"Why don't you think so?"

"Why the church? Hall didn't strike me as a churchgoing fellow. There were far better places to kill the girl and hide her. Why would he come into a strange town and kill his girlfriend somewhere where he knew she would be found? And if he then drove fifty miles to the gas station and bought gas just to try and establish an alibi, well..."

"You think he's innocent?"

"I think no one, not even the chief, can explain Walter's belt at the scene. He would have had to have gotten it from Walter's apartment, and how would he, a stranger in town, possibly know that?"

"He couldn't have," Kyle said, suddenly regaining his enthusiasm.

"I talked to Hall at the station and took him to identify the body. I didn't know him well, but he proclaimed his innocence, and I believed him."

Mae appeared at the door. The look on her face told Asa that she was impatient. "The church budget meeting is in ten minutes."

"Oh, I have to get my notes," Kyle said. "A couple of items I want to bring up..." And he went quickly out the door.

Mae stood looking at him, the way Asa's grandmother used to look at him.

"Hall is innocent, isn't he?"

"I can't prove it, Mae. There are questions beyond a reasonable doubt in my eyes."

"What are you going to do?"

"I'm going to go to the budget meeting," he answered. He squeezed past her and walked down the hall. He felt her gaze boring into him and resisted the urge to turn around.

In return for anointing someone to be a pastor, Asa believed God tempered that calling by requiring churches to have committees and making the pastor have to attend them. Scriptures spoke of hell as a fiery place where one is eternally separated from God, but sometimes Asa believed the sinners there were also forced to attend church committee meetings.

This was his first one as the new pastor, and he'd decided to see where the church finances stood, especially considering the recent issues.

Ninety minutes later, Asa and Kyle emerged from the conference room.

"Well, at least you got some extra money for the youth activities," Asa said.

"Thanks for supporting me on that," Kyle said.

Asa nodded. "If you can grow the youth ministry, maybe we can look at hiring a helper for you."

"That would be nice."

"Can I ask a question?"

"Sure," Kyle answered.

"Where did the old pastor and his arm candy run off to?"

Kyle shook his head. "Not sure. Some say they were headed to Vegas."

"A shame. The church is doing fine—better than I'd expected, honestly. We will weather this."

"I think having you here is already assuring the congregation."

Kyle stopped and put the stack of papers he was holding on the wall, took out a pen, and scribbled his name. "Almost forgot to sign in on the attendance sheet."

"Before you go," Asa said, "I need your help with something."

"Sure."

"Who would I go to in town for all the latest gossip?"

"Oh, that's easy. Georgeann. She runs the local beauty shop. Does my mom's hair."

"Is she in the know?"

Kyle grinned. "If it's happening in Glen Pines, Georgeann will know about it."

"Go talk to her or your mom. Find out anything and everything, especially if there are any hot romances going on around town."

"What are you thinking?"

"Not sure," Asa said. "Just a hunch."

Asa went back to his office and sat down. He was thinking about lunch when he picked up the phone.

"Doc? It's Asa Carter. Can I come down for a chat?"

DOC ADAMS MET ASA IN THE HALLWAY OF the M.E. building. The doctor had a cup of coffee in his hand and gestured for Asa to help himself to a cup.

"You look tired," Asa said.

"Two autopsies within a couple of weeks is a record for this town. Plus, I have an active practice."

"What did you find?"

"I haven't had a chance to contact the chief yet."

"Good. What did you find?"

Adams shot him a slight smile. "Your boy Hall died between eight p.m. and midnight from cardiac arrest caused by a gas embolism."

Asa paused, the coffee cup halfway to his mouth. "He injected himself with air?"

"Either Hall killed himself or someone else did it. There was no trace of heroin in that syringe," Doc said. "What tipped you off?"

"One, the lack of any evidence of drugs in the room. Plus the needle was in Hall's right arm," Asa said. "It occurred to me right before I called you, he was right-handed."

"How'd you know that?"

"I was at the station when he signed his statement," Asa said.

"Could he have been ambidextrous?"

"A possibility, but I didn't see any sign of it," Asa admitted. He sat down in a plastic chair and thought for a moment. "How about alcohol?"

"Oh, he was drunk as a skunk," Adams answered. "But not fatal levels, although he was probably passed out."

"Passed out when someone got in and put the needle in his arm," Asa said.

"Can't prove it definitively," Doc said. "Had there been traces of heroin in him or in the needle, I could chalk it up to an accident. Maybe he didn't clear the hypo of air before injection."

"But there was no residue."

"None," Adams said.

"I know something else," Asa said. "The chief is not going to like this."

CHAPTER TWENTY-EIGHT

MORE QUESTIONS THAN ANSWERS

DANIELS NEARLY LEAPED OUT OF HIS CHAIR. "You have got to be kidding me!"

Asa laid the coroner's report on the chief's desk. "Read it."

Daniels angrily picked up the folder and opened it. He read the report and slowly set the folder down. "The mayor's going to have my badge over this."

Asa sat and said nothing. There was little he could say, but he could sympathize. He'd once caught a case involving an extramarital affair by one of the city council's most popular men. He'd been leaned on by everyone, it seemed, to drop it and let it go. But he hadn't. And it had nearly cost him his badge.

Daniels leaned back and rubbed his eyes. "Maybe he should."

"Ned..."

"No, no," Daniels waved Asa's word aside. "You told me it was in the details, and I jumped the gun before the data came in."

"A rookie mistake," Asa said. "It happens."

"Two murders in this town and neither one solved, and what am I going to tell the mayor?"

"Wrong question," Asa said. "The question you should be asking is: Why was Hall murdered?"

"Why?"

"Good question. And one that needs an answer."

"Was it even the same person who murdered the girl?"

"Another good question, Chief." Asa leaned back. "Let's suppose—for the sake of argument—that it was the same person. Then the question becomes why. The only links Hall had to Tara Brooks were that they were both from the same region, both had a drug background, both had done a stint in rehab, *and* they were dating. Neither one had any direct connection to Glen Pines, so, again...why?"

"And if it wasn't the same person?"

"Then the case just got more complicated. Any evidence of robbery?"

"He had no money in his wallet," Daniels said. "But if I were the murderer, I'd try to make it look like a robbery. Wouldn't you?"

"I would. But a robber wouldn't have bothered to take the time to inject Hall with an air bubble. No, Chief, this wasn't a robbery. Hall was targeted."

Daniels let out a breath. "I don't even know where to start." He slammed his fist down on the desk. "We look like the f–frickin' Keystone Cops!" He looked at Asa. "You gotta help me. The department."

Asa rose. "I am."

"What are you going to do?"

"Start snooping," Asa said. "By the way...when Hall's truck tried to run me over?"

"Yeah."

"It was late…nearly eleven p.m." Asa tapped his temple. "Doc puts the time of death between ten and one. I think Hall was already dead, and the murderer was driving that truck."

Daniels was pondering that statement when Asa left. He felt like he was treading water, and it was up to his neck.

KYLE CAUGHT UP TO ASA AS HE WALKED across the church parking lot. "Hoo boy, did Georgeann give me an earful."

"That was quick."

"I figured you'd want it as fast as possible."

"So, what do you have?"

"Rumor has it that the mayor is having himself a fling when his wife's out of town."

"Any idea who that might be?"

"No. There are theories, of course, but she—Georgeann—says that they always get the same room at the motel."

"Really."

He nodded. "That's what she says. Also, widow Anderson has been driving to—"

Asa patted his arm. "That's good enough for now."

GAIL WAS BEHIND THE DESK WHEN ASA GOT to the motel.

"You're the preacher," she said.

"Asa Carter."

"Right. What brings you around?" She smiled. "I talked to a couple of ladies from your congregation. You used to be a cop."

"I was."

"Quite a change from being a pastor."

"Light years," Asa replied.

"That's why you knew about the warrant when you and the chief came in here the first time," she said.

"Let's talk about Jack Hall."

She shook her head. "Lord, two people killed, one in my own motel. Can you believe it?"

Now you know how I feel, Asa thought. "Anyone report hearing anything that night? Say around ten or after?"

"Lordy, I don't know. The office closes at ten. I was in the back doing the books."

"Did anyone come in? Any noises or anything unusual?"

She thought. "Nothing."

"The rooms on either side of his...either of them occupied by anyone that night?"

Gail looked as though she might blush. She diverted her gaze away.

"Gail..."

"I'm not supposed to say."

"Hindering a police investigation can be a felony," Asa said. "Now, you're not going to make me go and tell Chief Daniels that, are you?"

"One room was occupied that night. Fourteen."

The one next door to Hall's. "Are they still here?"

"Nah, they only rent it for a short time."

"Who?"

"Couple from town. They prefer to keep their fling...private."

"An affair?"

Gail spread her hands. "None of my business."

"They sign the register?"

"Of course, but under assumed names." She pressed some keys on the computer.

"John and Barb Smith," Asa said. "Hmmm."

"See? Private."

"I need their names, Gail. It's important."

Gail sighed. "They pay me good money to keep hush-hush."

"Well, maybe you could still help me another way," Asa said.

CHAPTER TWENTY-NINE

ASA MAKES A DISCOVERY

"HE ACTUALLY TOLD YOU TO BACK OFF?"

"Not exactly, but the implication was definitely there," Asa answered. He scooped steamed broccoli onto his plate. "He also implied without implying that if I stirred up the hornet's nest, Walter might get in more trouble. Again."

Ellen put a hand to her mouth. "Can he do that?"

"Who knows? Hall didn't kill that girl, and if he did, you're going to be hard-pressed to prove it to me." Asa twisted the top of the pepper grinder to flavor his pork chop. "Plus, there is this matter of the couple next to Hall's room the night he was killed. I'd like to talk to them, see if they heard or saw anything. But if Gail was right—"

"Who's Gail?"

"Manager of the motel. She says this couple has a tryst once a week, and that night they were there."

"Did she say who they were?"

Asa shook his head. "The man is married, and they sign in with aliases. The man gives Gail a nice sum every time to keep her trap shut, and she wants to respect that."

"Frustrating," Ellen said. "Isn't that hindering a police investigation?"

"It would be if there were actually an investigation," Asa answered. He finished his dinner and pushed the plate back. "Oh, honey, maybe I need to forget it and just stay in my lane."

"Maybe," Ellen said. "But you're not going to."

"Why shouldn't I?"

"Because someone killed those people and someone has to be made accountable."

"I know."

"And you're the only one who can do it."

He looked at his wife. "You just couldn't wait until I took my little pension and left the police and got full-time into the ministry. Now you're dragging me back in?"

"I'm not dragging you back to the police force. I'm telling you to use your God-given skills and knowledge and experience and find justice for them." Ellen put her fork down. "This may surprise you, Asa Carter, but I was proud of what you did. You were a good detective, and you cared for the families and friends who'd lost a loved one."

"Then why did you want me to leave?"

"Because the call to ministry was weighing on you, and you needed to make a choice. It would have been wrong for you to ignore the Lord's calling and stay a cop. The conflict was eating at you. You knew the decision you needed to make; you just needed a little push."

He smiled. "And you pushed."

"Maybe just a nudge," she admitted. "It didn't take much."

"No," Asa conceded. "It didn't."

She stood and began gathering their plates. "So, what are you going to do?"

"Gail is being paid to be discreet, so she didn't tell me who they were, but she did tell me when they made the next reservation and the room."

"You're going to spy?"

"In police terminology, it's called a stakeout, dear."

"And what happens when they show up? Are you going to confront them?"

"I'm thinking about it."

She bent down and kissed his cheek. "While you're thinking, help me with the dishes."

TWO NIGHTS LATER, ASA SAT IN HIS CAR AND kept an eye on the motel parking lot and his watch. Beside him, Kyle sat like a kid expecting a treat.

"This is so exciting." He opened a thermos and poured coffee into the plastic cup.

"I'm glad you think so," Asa said.

"Oh, come on, you must have done a hundred of these."

"And never really liked any of them," Asa said. "It was just the only way to nab the bad guys. And I wouldn't do that."

"Do what?"

"Drink so much coffee. Where are you going to pee?"

Kyle paused. "Guess I never thought about that." Disappointed, he poured the coffee back into the container. "Are we gonna arrest whoever shows up?"

"Not that we could, but why would we?"

"Well..." Kyle's shoulders slumped. "I thought we would be arresting someone."

"Sorry, kid. But coming along was your idea."

Gail said the couple had wanted the same room, and she always made sure they got it. One of the perks of being in a small town like Glen Pines was that there were few tourists, so the motel was never too busy.

A dark gray Nissan pulled into the slot in front of the room, and a woman got out. At first, they couldn't see her; but then she turned, scanning the parking lot suspiciously. She didn't look happy. She unlocked the door and disappeared inside.

"I don't believe it," Kyle breathed.

"Well, well," Asa spoke softly to the windshield. "Hello, Officer Reed."

"Who is she meeting?" Kyle whispered.

"Whoever she's meeting, she doesn't look happy about it," Asa said. Reed didn't have the anticipatory energy one might exhibit upon meeting a lover. She looked almost—scared. So, Asa wondered, who could it be?

He didn't have to wait long. A tan short-bed pickup, gleaming in the parking-lot lights and apparently recently washed and waxed, pulled in alongside Reed's Nissan. A long moment passed before the door opened. The figure also looked around. He tapped on the motel-room door, and it opened from the inside to let him in.

Asa whistled. "And hello, Mr. Mayor."

"Oh, wow," Kyle said. "Georgeann was right."

Asa sat back and thought for a moment, then started the car and pulled away. Time to go home. Something was beginning to jell in his mind, like a cloud coalescing into something firmer. He couldn't grab it yet, but a kernel was there.

"I gotta pee," Kyle said.

CHAPTER THIRTY

THE RUMOR MILL AND A VISITOR COMES

It was a simple service, held early in the afternoon when the sun was bright and warm. Asa had expected few mourners, because Tara Brooks wasn't from around here; but, to his surprise, two dozen of his parishioners and almost the same number from Father Quinn's flock attended, gathering around the grave. Asa also recognized Marty, the owner of the Red Oak, and Kay, who had considered Tara a friend.

Asa read from the 23rd Psalm, and Quinn read from John Eleven where Jesus raised Lazarus and proclaimed to Martha and Mary that He was the resurrection and the life. Prayers were given, and the body of Tara Brooks was lowered into her resting place.

It was not the first funeral Asa had done. He had done plenty over his two decades. Some were those who'd been really ill, who had known their time was near. Others had been more sudden.

But a few had been quick and tragic and made little sense. And, Asa had admitted only to himself, not fair. Like Tara Brooks.

She may have made a mistake, but she had paid for it. And dying in a small town far from her home with no clue as to why, buried in that same town and mourned by people who barely knew her? It didn't seem fair.

But life, as Asa had often told his daughter and flock, was never fair. The Lord had never said life would be fair—quite the opposite, actually.

People came to him, offering their thanks for a well-done service and saying how pretty and moving it had been, and Asa accepted their praises with a meek smile. He glanced over to see Chief Daniels and Carla Reed in attendance, along with a couple of the other officers. Asa excused himself and walked to meet them.

"Mighty nice, Reverend," Daniels said. "Maybe she can rest now."

"What about Hall's body?" Reed asked.

"Claimed by a family member," Asa answered. "Took him back home, as far as I know."

One of the officers—Greene, Asa recalled his name was—kept glancing at him as though trying to get his attention. Asa shook his hand.

"Officer Greene, isn't it?"

"Yes, sir. You did a nice job."

"Thank you."

"Must be hard to eulogize someone you don't know very well."

"It can be a task," Asa admitted.

"Well..." Greene looked over at the chief, who was engaged

in a conversation with someone. "Can I come by your house tonight, or would I be imposing?"

"Not at all. Anything the matter?"

"You might say it's a spiritual matter of sorts."

"I see," Asa nodded. "Seven?"

Greene gave a tight smile. "Thanks."

KYLE FOUND ASA WHILE HE WAS WORKING IN his back yard in one of Ellen's flower gardens.

"Hey."

"You look excited," Asa said. "What's up?"

"Talked to Georgeann some more. Just wanted to see if she had any further details on the tryst."

"What made you do that?"

"Seeing Carla—Officer Reed—like that, well, it made me wonder, so I thought I'd try to get more out of her. Georgeann's not sure if his wife knows and doesn't care, or doesn't want to know. Something else. She said she heard that it might not be totally consensual."

"What do you mean?"

"She told me, whoever the person is, well, they're being sorta roped into the whole thing."

That would explain Reed's countenance at the motel, Asa thought.

Kyle scratched his head. "Wonder how he'd do that?"

"Blackmail is my first guess," Asa said. What could Carla Reed have done to leave her open to blackmail?

"Excuse me, but I don't know how this helps solve the murders," Kyle said, scratching his head.

"Me either. Yet." Asa put the plants into the hole and began to fill it in. "Thanks, Kyle."

He filled in the hole and sat there for a long moment. He needed to do something, but wasn't sure how he was going to do it.

They had just finished dinner, and Asa had retreated to his study on the pretext of working on a lesson for the midweek Bible study. He was still working on his problem, and it was circling in his head like a chess puzzle, full of possibilities that led nowhere. He was beginning to realize that there was no clear way to do it when he heard the doorbell and glanced at his watch.

He'd forgotten. Officer Greene was here.

CHAPTER THIRTY-ONE

GREENE HAS NEWS

ELLEN SHOWED GREENE INTO THE STUDY after offering him something to drink. Greene accepted her iced tea, which she left to get.

"This is nice," Greene said.

"Thank you."

"My father was a professor, if you can believe that. Thirty-five years. He had a study a lot like this. A place where he said he could read and think. *True men have a study*, he used to say," Greene said with a slight smile. "No man caves for him."

"What did he teach?"

"Ancient history."

"And I take it you didn't want to pursue that," Asa said.

"To be honest, Reverend, I hated history. Always did, much to his disappointment."

"A shame. There's a lot to learn about the present from the past."

"You sound like my father."

Ellen appeared with his tea and quietly closed the door behind her.

"So, what can I do for you, Officer Greene?"

"It's Timothy. You can call me Tim. I'm not here as a cop. Well, officially, anyway. Sort of, yeah, but—" He shook his head as though trying to ward off the wild train of thought. He sighed. "I don't know. I know you used to be a cop. And you might understand."

"Why don't you tell me about it?"

Greene fidgeted a little. "Reverend, I don't think Hall killed her."

"Have you told the chief that?"

"Yeah, but the mayor is on him big-time, and he seems resigned to drop it, but I don't think he's happy about it."

Asa resisted the urge to high-five him. "What makes you say that?"

"There's something...not right about this whole thing."

"Such as?"

"Walter's belt, for example. I've known Walter for nearly five years. He's a little slow on some things, yeah, but he wouldn't do that."

"You mean leave his belt there if he killed her with it?"

"Yeah. It seems a little too neat. And the bracelet in his place—I don't think that was the victim's. Even Hall said it was cheap."

"I see."

"But the thing I really don't get is that really, when you look at it, we have nothing. We have several suspects—Walter, Cobb, even Violet Corbin. I stopped her at the church that night. And sometimes she can be kinda creepy."

"And how about Hall?"

"A suspect, I suppose, and maybe he or Cobb could have picked the lock to get in. But everyone's acting like it's a solved case."

"And that bugs you."

"It does," Greene admitted. "Anyway, I guess I just wanted to vent my frustrations to someone, however crazy they might be."

"I don't think they're crazy," Asa said. "I don't think Hall killed her, either."

It was as though a load had suddenly lifted off the young cop. "So, what happens?"

"I'm going to find out who did," Asa said. "And if I need your help, maybe without Ned knowing it, could I count on you?"

"Sure. And not a word to the chief, please."

"Not a word to anyone, Tim," Asa said. "If anyone asks, you saw me about a spiritual matter."

Tim got up. "Thank you." He got to the door. "This is a small town, Reverend, but there's a lot of secrets here, I think. Secrets that might make people kill if they came to light."

"Thanks for coming by," Asa said.

The young cop left and Asa sat back, looking at the photo. He reached for the phone and called a number he hadn't used in over a decade.

WHEN HE CAME OUT OF THE STUDY, HE found Ellen reading in her favorite chair.

"Who were you talking to?"

"My girlfriend," Asa said. "Our date is off for tonight."

"Too bad," Ellen said. "Looks like you're stuck with me, then."

He leaned down and kissed her. "Ty."

"Ty Benson?"

"*Captain* Benson now," Asa said.

"A long way from a rookie detective."

"That it is."

"No surprise. You taught him, after all."

"A sharp cookie," Asa said. "And a good cop. I figured he'd go far."

"What's he doing?"

"Doing me a favor," Asa said. He sat down in his recliner, separated from her chair by a small square table. "I need to see everything on Tara Brooks's case."

"The DUI manslaughter?"

"The very same. Ty's going to contact the state cops and get the info and send it to me."

"Wouldn't that be public record?"

"Yeah, but I'd like to get the scoop from the cops who handled it. Sometimes there are impressions, hunches, things that don't always make it into the file." He sat back. "Something's just out of my reach on this case, Ell. I can't quite grab it yet, but I think I'm close."

"You think the case file will help?"

"Can't hurt. I think there's a link between what happened back then and her appearance here in Glen Pines."

"But what?"

"Don't know. Maybe that case file can tell me."

"Daniels could have gotten it for you, I'm sure."

"Daniels is sidelined by politics. The mayor wants this buried; and if Daniels wants to keep his job, he'll stamp it solved and move on." Asa sat down. "Greene came to me venting his concerns about the case. He's got good instincts. He'd make a good detective someday. He said this town has a lot of secrets."

"I could have told you that."

"Secrets that people might kill for?" Asa asked.

Ellen raised her eyebrow, her way of saying *Are you kidding?* "Maybe they just did."

CHAPTER THIRTY-TWO

TRUTHS ARE DISCOVERED

IT HAPPENED TO HIM SOMETIMES IN THE MOST unlikely places and at the most unlikely times. Once, it happened to him in the middle of a speech by the Chicago Police Commissioner. Asa had nearly bolted out of his chair when the solution of who'd killed an upscale stockbroker popped into his head. The Commissioner, knee-deep into his spiel, was totally unaware that something in an off-the-cuff remark he'd just made to the mayor's PR lady had helped solve a murder that had been dogging the department for nearly a month.

This one happened in his office with the door open, the ambient sound of Mae on the phone talking to someone, and one of Matthew Henry's Bible commentaries open before him. Asa paused and leaned back and dialed a number.

"Tim, it's Asa Carter. Remember you said I could count on you? Well, I need you to do something for me."

It was an easy request, and the officer agreed immediately. Asa thanked him and hung up. He buzzed Mae into his office and shut the door.

"What is it?"

"Something you might not believe," he said.

THIRTY MINUTES LATER, ASA STOOD WITH Tim Greene at the local jewelry shop. Greene had the bracelet taken from Walter's apartment and had removed it from the evidence bag.

"The chief will have my butt for this."

"He'll thank us later," Asa said.

The jeweler looked at it.

"Nah, this isn't expensive. These sell at the big box retail places. Twenty, thirty bucks most likely."

Hall had been right. Asa asked "You don't sell them here?"

"Nothing that cheap," the jeweler answered. "Now, if you are thinking of one for the wife..."

Asa smiled. "Later, perhaps. Any place in town that would sell them?"

"Yeah, one place that I know of."

THE MANAGER OF THE LOCAL DEPARTMENT store met Asa in his office. "You want to know what?"

Asa showed him a photo of the bracelet. "You sell these?"

"Sure."

"To anyone in particular?"

"Not really. I've had one particularly good customer in the past three months."

"Who is that?"

"Hmmm, I don't know. Just that someone's been buying them."

"You got sales receipts?"

"Come on, Pastor, this is the modern age. Everything is electronic. The old days of that are gone. I can tell you when they were sold, but not who bought them."

"But you do have cameras on your jewelry counters?" Asa asked.

"Well, yes."

"Could I see the footage?"

"There's a lot of it."

Asa smiled. "I'll fast-forward through the slow parts."

WALTER CAME INTO THE OFFICE. "YOU wanted to see me?"

"Yeah, I did." Asa motioned at the door. "Shut it, please. I need to talk to you about something important."

"Okay," Walter said. "I guess I never got to say thank you for getting me out. My lawyer says I might have to go back to court." He sat on the sofa.

"Maybe, but there's a chance you won't," Asa said. "I know you didn't kill Tara Brooks."

Walter grinned. "That's good."

"But you did lie to me, Walter. And Chief Daniels—and, worst of all, to Mae."

For a moment the big man's eyes widened. He opened his mouth, and Asa held up a hand. "That bracelet we found in your apartment. True, it wasn't Tara's. It was yours. You bought it at Brookdale Department Store five days before Tara's murder. I saw you on their security-camera footage. You bought it for someone special. Someone who likes bracelets. You bought it for Violet."

Walter hung his head. "How did you find out?"

"I was a detective, Walter. We find things out." Asa went over and sat beside him and put an arm around him. "Violet's been seen hanging around the church a lot lately in the evenings when it gets dark. She's been coming to see you, hasn't she?"

Walter nodded. "She didn't want anyone to know. She made me promise not to tell anyone."

"Why?"

"She was afraid that people might try to stop us." Walter looked up and there were tears in his eyes. "So was I."

"Why would they do that?"

"Because I'm...you know."

"So you didn't tell. Not even to Mae."

"I—I'm sorry, Pastor. I just made Violet a promise." He wiped his eyes. "Nothing happened, Pastor Asa. Not that stuff. We just hung out and watched TV." He hung his head again. "She's nice to me."

"I'm glad she is." Asa leaned in. "Do you like her?"

"Yes."

He patted the janitor on his broad back. "It's okay, big guy. Men have done crazier things than that for a woman."

"Really?"

"Really. But I think you need to tell Mae."

"Do I have to?"

"Normally, no. You're a grown-up and you don't need to tell anyone about your personal life, but you did lie to her, Walter. And to the police and me. You need to make it right."

"I suppose."

"What would your mom have had you do?"

He sighed. "Tell the truth."

"Okay. There's your answer."

"I'm scared."

"Doing the right thing isn't always easy, buddy," Asa said. "But you're brave, and you can do it. Your momma taught you that."

"She did." He stood up, and Asa had to look up at him. The tears were gone. "I'm sorry, Pastor Asa, that I lied to you."

"Accepted." He motioned to the door. "Go talk to Mae."

Walter nodded, and the door shut behind him.

CHAPTER THIRTY-THREE

THE FRIEND

"IMAGINE THAT BOY AFRAID TO TELL ME THAT he has a girlfriend," Mae said. She stood in the doorway.

"I don't think he views that term like you or I might," Asa said. "They're just friends."

"You don't buy a bracelet for just a friend," Mae retorted. "But it clears him of murder."

"Not entirely. There's still the matter of his belt. If he didn't leave it up there, how did it get up there?"

"Two of the suspects are good at lock picking, mind you," Mae said. "Getting into his apartment wouldn't be hard."

She had a point. But one of the lock-picking people was dead. Violet had been ruled out, not that Asa felt she had anything much to do with it. So that left Cobb.

"I can't see Cobb going to all that trouble, breaking into someone's place and stealing a belt," Asa said. "He'd probably use his own and take it with him. Or toss it. Cobb wouldn't leave it at the scene. Even he's not that stupid."

Mae snorted. "Could have fooled me. That man's been trouble since he was born. And there is his temper."

Asa got up. "I'm going out."

"Who are you going to talk to?"

"Just hold down the fort, Mae."

"As if I never do," she said.

HE WALKED INTO THE FLOWER SHOP TO FIND Violet near the counter. "Hi, Violet."

She didn't look at him. "Hello."

The owner of the shop—whose name Asa couldn't recall—looked at him, and Asa identified himself. "I need to speak to Violet for a moment in private, please. Shouldn't take a minute." He walked behind the counter and into the back room.

"You know why I'm here?" Asa asked.

"You think I killed that girl," Violet said.

"I don't think you killed that girl," Asa said. "You know that."

She gave a small nod.

"It's okay, Violet. I know."

"Know what?"

"About you and Walter."

Her eyes widened and Asa held out a reassuring hand. "It's all right. I don't care that you come over and hang out with him. He even went to jail because the police thought the bracelet belonged to the dead girl. He'd bought it for you earlier, and he lied rather than spill your secret. He was honoring your wish."

"I'm sorry, Pastor..."

"It's okay," Asa said. "But I need the truth now, Violet. Two people are dead, and I need to find justice for them."

"W–what do you need?"

"That night of the murder, when you say that you heard arguing, remember?"

"Yes."

"Coming from inside the church?"

"Yes."

"Did you see any cars in the parking lot?"

"Just the police car."

"You mean when Officer Greene talked to you?"

She shook her head. "No, before that."

"There was a police car in the parking lot?"

"Yes."

"Was it Officer Greene's car?"

"I don't know."

"You didn't notice the number?"

"Number?"

"All police cars have a number on them, so you can tell them apart."

She shook her head. "No, I didn't notice."

"When did it leave?"

"It was there when I left. I heard the yelling and I hurried away."

"Thank you, Violet," Asa said.

"I'm sorry," she said.

"You've got nothing to be sorry for."

"Can Walter and I still be friends?"

"Of course," Asa said. "See him any time you want."

Violet smiled. "Pastor?"

"Yes?"

"There's something else."

CHAPTER THIRTY-FOUR

THE REVELATION

THE EMAIL ARRIVED WITH A SMALL NOTE AND a Kentucky phone number. Soon, Asa had Sheriff Grant Durbin on the phone.

"I was surprised to get a call from Chicago. Your friend Captain Benson was pretty persuasive. He says you were a Chicago cop once."

"Once," Asa said. "I helped train Benson when he got his gold shield. I'm a pastor now and we have a dead girl here. Tara Brooks."

"Oh, yeah, I remember Tara. That's been a while. How'd she die?"

"Strangled," Asa said. "Police force is small and inexperienced. I'm just serving as an adviser of sorts."

"Any suspects?"

"Her boyfriend was here too."

"Hall?"

"You know him?"

"Yeah, they were an item when she got out. How's he?"

"Dead."

"Wow. You think he killed her?"

"No," Asa said. "But somebody wants me to think that. I think it's tied to what happened with her DUI case. It's a hunch, but it's the only thing at this point that would make sense. What happened?"

"The victim was a forty-year-old male, local farmer, well-known, churchgoer too. Just crushed him. Never knew what hit him, poor guy. Tara Brooks was found at the scene in the driver's seat, passed out."

"Hall said that Tara claimed there was someone else in the car with her."

"Yeah. Her best friend, Carrie Anderson. She claimed that Carrie was driving. When the cops arrived, there was just Tara in the car."

"Did they question Carrie?"

"Tried to. But her dad was an attorney here in town. Very powerful. She had an ironclad alibi, and the prosecutor at the time didn't want to take on Adams very hard. That was a good way to ruin a career."

"What happened?"

"Tara gets convicted, pleads to DUI manslaughter, and gets ten."

"And Carrie Anderson?"

"Well, the old man died of cancer two years after it happened. Carrie vanished and has never come back."

"Any idea where she went?"

"Nope. Rumor has it the old man knew he was dying and that his enemies—and he had lots of them, believe me—might come after his daughter when he could no longer protect her. He supposedly gave her a whole new identity—name change, the works—and sent her packing."

"Sounds like she might have been guilty."

"I was just a deputy here then, but I thought she was. Proving it here in this town is another story."

"Any idea on what she changed the name to?"

"He didn't get it done here, obviously," Durbin answered. "And after he died and the daughter vanished, people pretty much forgot about it."

"And Tara being sent to jail."

"Yeah." Durban paused. "So, what does this have to do with her ending up dead there?"

"I think the former Carrie Anderson is living here and Tara came here to confront her," Asa said. "Boyfriend said Tara told him she was wanting redemption."

"Hard to get if you kill someone," Durbin said.

Asa couldn't argue with him there. He hung up and sat lost in thought for a long moment. Ellen came in. "Did you find out anything?"

"Tara Brooks was framed by her best friend for the manslaughter charge, I think."

"That's sad. She had a tough life."

"Lots of people do, honey."

"Still, it can leave scars that sometimes all the faith in the world can't fully erase," Ellen continued. "I see that every day in the eyes of students." She leaned down and kissed his cheek. "I love you."

He smiled and squeezed her hand.

She walked out, and Asa sat for a long moment staring at the corner. Suddenly, his head came up.

"Hey..."

He thought for a moment more. “Hey…” Louder now.

Ellen appeared at the door again, and Asa was hunched over his desk, looking at something. “Get me a magnifying glass, honey.”

“Asa, what in…” Her voice trailed off as she went into the kitchen. Asa sat staring at the photo of the two young girls. Ellen handed him the glass and he pored over the photo.

“Asa…”

He suddenly straightened. “‘Ask and ye shall receive.’”

“What?”

“I know who killed her, baby.”

“Please tell me it wasn’t Walter.”

“No,” Asa said, “it wasn’t.”

“You don’t look happy.”

He leaned back with a sigh. “Now I have to prove it.”

CHAPTER THIRTY-FIVE

DANIELS MAKES A DECISION

THE HOUSE WAS A TWO-STORY FRAME SET BEtween twin oak trees. A front porch held a swing and a rocking chair that reminded Asa of the one his mother had once had. He walked up the steps to the door and rang the bell. Chief Daniels opened it and stood staring for a heartbeat.

"This is a surprise, Reverend."

"I need a moment, Ned, if I can."

A middle-aged woman peered around the chief's large frame.

"This is my wife, Rose."

Asa nodded. "A pleasure, Mrs. Daniels. I'm Reverend Carter."

She smiled. "I've heard a lot about you. Your wife is a darling."

Daniels interjected. "Rose teaches at the high school too."

"Even nicer," Asa said.

"Rose, the good reverend and I will be on the porch."

She nodded, the same acquiescent look that Ellen had in situations where her husband needed privacy.

Asa chose the porch swing and Daniels took a wooden rocker. "This about the murders?"

"I know who killed them, Ned."

"Really? Care to share it with me?"

"No, because I know the mayor has you tied up." Asa held up a hand. "Relax; I'm not blaming you. Politics have interfered with police work since the dawn of man. I just need you to make a couple of phone calls for me."

"To who—whom?" Daniels waved it off. "Never can keep that straight."

"State police, CID unit."

"You bringing in the state boys on me, Asa?"

"No. But I need their expertise. Also, I need the lab reports from Hall's crime scene."

"I don't honestly know if we've gotten them back yet."

"Okay, they can help me out with that too."

Daniels sighed. "I don't know..."

"Ned, there comes a time in the life of any cop who leads other cops when he has to decide if he's a cop first or a politician first." Asa stood up. "Two people are dead, both of whom never deserved their fate, flawed and imperfect as they might have been. I just laid Tara Brooks to rest. Someone needs to speak for her, Ned. That's what you and everyone does who works a homicide. We speak for the dead since they can't. Since I got here, people have been telling me what a good man you are. Honest and fair. Well, Chief, are you? Are you the Chief of Police, or are you a puppet of the mayor? I can solve this case, but I need your help. Just a lousy phone call, Ned."

Slowly, Daniels's head nodded. "Okay, Rev, I'll call my contact over there, give him your number. Any word gets to the mayor—"

"Not a word to anyone, Chief. Not even to the other officers."

Daniels looked up at Asa. "I have a bad feeling about this."

"Relax," Asa said. "If I'm right, things will be right as rain before you know it."

"And if you're wrong?"

"Then we never had this conversation." Asa stepped off the porch. "But I'm not."

SERGEANT ISAAC MALLORY WAS AN INVESTIGAtor with the state police's Criminal Investigation Division. He showed up at the church two days later and, when he flashed a badge at Mae, the elderly woman walked as fast as she could into Asa's office.

"Pastor, there's...someone from the state police here to see you."

"Offer him coffee, Mae, then send him in."

Mallory was of medium height and solidly built. He had apparently declined Mae's coffee and walked slightly hesitatingly into Asa's office. Asa stood.

"Reverend Carter?"

"Sergeant Mallory, a pleasure. Please sit."

The cop was experienced; Asa watched his eyes flicker across the certificates on the wall behind Asa. "Ned Daniels said you were homicide in Chicago."

"That's right."

"Says you're a straight-up guy."

"Given my current profession, I certainly hope so."

Mallory's hard exterior cracked with a slight smile before he laid a thick folder on the desk. "Here is what you asked for, although I was surprised to see that they never looked at their copy of the lab results. You were right about the print, though. It was a partial, and we ran it through the state database and came back with a hit. My bosses are clamoring for me to step in."

"You will, I assure you," Asa said. "But first things first. Did you do the other checks?"

"I did. They're all there."

Asa scanned through them.

While he did, Mallory said, "I'd like to know your theory, as well as your solution."

"Oh, don't worry," Asa said. "You're going to get it. About the fingerprint..."

"About that," Mallory said. "That was an even bigger surprise."

"What do you mean?"

Mallory told him, and Asa had to laugh.

"What's so funny?"

"I've been thickheaded, that's what's funny. I should have seen it."

"Care to share it with me?"

Asa did.

CHAPTER THIRTY-SIX

ASA EXPLAINS IT ALL

HE HELD THE MEETING IN THE WORSHIP CENter of Grace Gospel Church. Mae was there, sitting alongside Walter, who fidgeted a little in the pew. Violet sat on Walter's other side, blushing slightly under the occasional curious glance. Cobb muttered, upon entering, that he found churches creepy; but he sat down dutifully, under the watchful eye of several officers, including Greene and Carla Reed, who kept a close, but respectful, distance.

At last, Chief Daniels came in, alongside the mayor.

"Really, Chief, you need to explain yourself, with all this."

"Just sit down, Ron. Everything will be explained."

"You could tell me."

"I don't know all the details myself," Daniels said. "So we'll find out together."

"Did you catch the murderer, or not?" Foster asked as he sat down, across the aisle from the rest of the audience.

Asa walked onto the stage and went to the pulpit. With him

was someone, unknown to everyone else, who sat in the chair behind the pulpit, which was usually reserved for the senior pastor.

"Thank you all for coming," Asa said, and gestured to Mallory. "This is Sergeant Mallory of the State Police Criminal Investigation Division. He has been so kind as to assist in this case."

"Have you caught the killer, or not?" Ron Foster called out.

Asa ignored him. "Well, once upon a time in a little town in Kentucky there were two little girls, lifelong friends. One was from the lower economic rung, and the other had a father who was an attorney—a powerful local figure who practically ruled the town. But he also made enemies. After all, one doesn't get to be that powerful without making some enemies along the way.

"Now, these two girls grew up together and, as teens do, they partied and they made mistakes. One night they drank too much and tried to drive home. Out on the highway, they hit a man and killed him. Now, in the crash, poor Tara Brooks was knocked out, but it was her friend CC—Carrie Cecille Anderson—who was driving. CC had an idea. She put her best friend in the driver's seat and fled the scene. By the time the cops arrived, Tara was coming to, and no amount of insistence could convince anyone that CC had been driving—because CC's father squashed any sort of inquiry into the whole business. And Tara Brooks took a plea of ten years and went to prison.

"In the next few years, Mr. Anderson is dying. His enemies smell blood and are circling; and he knows that once he's gone, he might not be able to protect his daughter from them. So the lawyer comes up with a radical solution: He gives his daughter a new identity—name and everything. Carrie Anderson disappears forever, and the father makes sure that any records of the name change are buried. And Carrie moves away and begins a new life.

"Years pass, and Tara Brooks gets out of prison. She's served her time, but the wounds are fresh and she wants one thing. Jack Hall says she was wanting redemption. Not because she was guilty, but because she was innocent. So, Tara finds her long-lost friend, right here in Glen Pines." Asa held up a finger. "Now, that answers a question: Why did Tara Brooks come to Glen Pines when she had no connection to the place? Everyone assumed, including me, that she came here to start over and rebuild her life. And perhaps that was true, but it was not the real reason. She came here because her old friend was here, living under a new name, a new life. She came here and contacted the girl she had once known as CC. I think it was a shock. Imagine CC's surprise to suddenly one day see your best friend from your former life working in the local diner. I can't imagine the shock, fear, and panic that might have hit her. How did Tara know CC was here? We'll get back to that.

"In addition, Tara was being hounded by an amorous fellow whose life of petty crime and drug abuse had sealed his fate in never getting Tara Brooks on a date. He even threatened her in his anger and frustration. In fact, she was still very much in love with Mr. Hall, from all that we have discovered.

"But someone else knew CC's secret. Knew about her former life, the DUI, and even helped her get training and a job. But there was a price to be paid. This person began to blackmail CC, forcing her into a sexual relationship. The arrival of Tara Brooks threatened the blackmail and threatened to upend CC's new life.

"The two former friends were seen talking in the diner and once out on the street. Tara was hostile on the last visit, and I was told Tara was upset that a background check had been done on her. But that wasn't what she was angry about.

"So, CC takes her to the church, somewhere quiet, somewhere that they can be totally alone. I know this because Tara's motorcycle was not in the parking lot, but still at the motel. Picking the lock, CC takes her inside, where they talk—and it spirals into an argument. I know that because someone was in the parking lot and overheard the argument coming from inside. The fact that this person was there was also mysterious, but it turns out that this witness had a valid reason for being at the church at that hour."

He saw Violet blush. Walter took her hand. Everyone was quiet.

"Tempers flare as the argument grows louder. The killer, formerly known as CC, grabs the belt hanging near the folding table and strangles Tara Brooks and leaves her face down in the water. The killer hides the belt behind some things and leaves the church. But in the struggle—because Tara Brooks puts up a struggle—the killer drops this." Asa held up the earring. "But we'll come back to that.

"I assumed that the slight tan line on Tara Brooks's wrist was an indication of a bracelet that had fallen off in the struggle or was taken by the killer. She wore only expensive bracelets, according to Mr. Hall, her boyfriend. But remember, Tara had just left a halfway house, and an expensive bracelet in such an environment would have been a target for a lot of people. But what if she had gotten out and bought one? A possibility; but if she was wearing one, the bracelet was not at the scene. And there was none found in her motel room. There *was* a bracelet found in Walter Pence's apartment. Again, it was a cheap one, purchased by Mr. Pence himself as a gift. That has been confirmed through security video at the store where he bought it. So that was not Tara's.

"But she did have one. Two days before she died, Tara Brooks gave that nice bracelet to someone. Someone who reminded Tara a little bit of herself. A lost soul, if you will. And to apologize to her because of an argument they'd had earlier. You see, Tara had been accused of being interested in this woman's boyfriend. She wasn't, but when the argument happened, Tara realized how much this woman cared about her guy, so she gave her the bracelet. It was a present from a woman to another woman in Tara's attempt to help this person look better for the guy she was interested in. She gave it to Violet Corbin."

All eyes turned toward the meek woman, who held her arm in the air and pointed to one of the bracelets on her wrist. She blushed and quickly lowered her hand.

"Now, there was the question of Walter Pence's belt and if he could have been the murderer. In fact, the belt was left there, but Walter didn't leave it there—Violet did, when she did his laundry two days earlier."

Walter turned to her. "I didn't know that."

She smiled. "I wanted to surprise you, but I'm sorry I forgot your belt. I'd taken it off of your pants and I'd forgotten all about it."

Asa went on. "Anyway, the night of the murder, Violet heard the argument as she was coming home from Walter's place. But that's not all. Violet saw two police cars that night. One was when Officer Greene—" Asa pointed to the young cop in the back of the room "—stopped her to ask her what she was doing in the parking lot. A routine security stop." He held up a finger.

"But there was another police car that night, parked there at the time of the murder, seen there while she heard the argument. The car driven by the killer, by CC." He now looked at the back. "Isn't that right, Officer Reed?"

All eyes turned. Carla Reed froze for a moment, then pointed a finger. "You're crazy, Rev. I didn't kill anyone!"

"It was your car there," Asa said. "And how do I know this?" He held up the photo he'd taken from Tara's room. "This picture taken from Tara's motel room. Tara Brooks at ten years old with her best friend CC, the identities verified by Sgt. Mallory through their school photos. Now, that itself doesn't prove much, but this does." He held up another photograph, a blowup showing an arm.

"See that? A scar, running down CC's forearm, received when the girl went through a sliding glass door. Just like the one on your arm, Officer Reed."

Reed whirled and froze. Three state troopers stood behind her. One of them reached down and removed her sidearm.

"Daddy changed your name," Asa said. "He didn't think to change the scar."

"Please don't move," the trooper said to a sulking Carla Reed.

CHAPTER THIRTY-SEVEN

THE MURDER OF JACK HALL

"NOW, IF I MAY CONTINUE," ASA SAID. "WE come to the murder of Tara's boyfriend, Jack Hall. Hall died not of an overdose, as was reported, but by air injected into his veins, resulting in a fatal embolism. Hall was right-handed, which made it odd that he would have injected himself with his left hand. People almost always use the dominant hand to inject, so how could this have happened? Well, the killer must have thought that Hall was left-handed. When Jack Hall was released from questioning, he'd forgotten to sign his statement, and Chief Daniels made him sign it on the front counter." He glanced at Daniels sitting in the front row with the mayor.

"Remember that, Chief?"

Daniels nodded. "I do."

"Now the station's front lobby can be observed by anyone sitting in the cubicles where the officers' desks are. A large mirror gives them clear views of anyone and anything in the lobby in case there is trouble. Am I right, Chief?"

"Correct as well," Daniels said.

"The problem is, a mirror reverses the image, you see. When Hall signed his statement, anyone looking at it through the mirror would see Hall signing with his left hand—not his right. Officer Reed was there when Hall was released, and she observed the whole thing. Which would explain the mistake on the needle."

"I didn't kill Jack Hall!" Reed shouted, having to be restrained by the troopers. "I didn't!"

"No, you didn't," Asa said. "But you were in the room next door with your blackmailer, the one forcing you to have a sexual relationship or he would blow your secret. The same person I spoke to across a table and caught a faint whiff of perfume. The same perfume I smell on you every time I'm around you. And he was the one who convinced you that Hall also needed to go, that it would be a perfect solution to the town's problem. Hall dies, he gets the blame, everyone walks away. But you told him that Hall was left-handed and to inject the hypo into the right arm." Asa turned to Mayor Foster. "You were a teacher once. Your prints are in a database. You left a partial thumbprint on the plunger." Asa drew out another photo and held it up. "I took that the last time you two were at the motel."

"Idiot!" Reed screamed.

"No wonder you were the first officer on the scene when the chief and I found him dead. You were right next door, just where you'd been all night. Except—" Asa raised a finger. "When you were driving Hall's truck and tried to scare me with that lame attempt to run me over. You even hit the flower bed, as though Hall was driving drunk. A nice touch, to be sure. But Hall wasn't driving. He was dead already, killed by the mayor, and he made you do the truck thing to try and cover your tracks."

"You can't prove that."

"You left a print on the steering wheel," Mallory said.

Foster got up in indignation and started to leave, but Daniels grabbed his arm and nodded. A state trooper came down, and Foster sat again.

"Miss Reed, I suggest you make no further statements until you have an attorney present," Asa said. "By the way, we found photos in your apartment showing you wearing the earrings that match the one left at the church. We found them when Sergeant Mallory and the troopers here in the church executed a search warrant of your apartment. And there was only one of them in your jewelry box."

He turned to the mayor. "You knew she'd killed Tara. You knew she did it, and you never said anything. Because in your eyes, Tara was better off dead rather than get the chance to blab what she knew to who knows who. But one thing I don't know: How did you know who Carla Reed really was when she came here?"

"My father..." Foster sighed. "He worked for a law firm in Indiana. I remember it very well. Took the whole firm to pull it off, and Anderson spared no expense. New birth certificate, everything. Used the one from some poor baby that had died."

"And one day here she comes, riding into Glen Pines, looking for a job," Asa said. "And you know it is her. Your father helped change her identity, and you were a witness those years ago. What are the odds that she comes here? You help her with the minimum amount of training for her certification, get her on the police department. But there was a price."

"Yeah," Reed spoke up. "I didn't want Hall killed. He didn't know anything about me." She glared at Foster. "But you had to protect your secret affair, didn't you?"

"Want to tell me how Tara found you, Carla? You have the right to remain silent."

The officer rolled her eyes. "She was smarter than I thought. Told me it took her two years of sorting through databases from prison and contacting my father's old enemies back home. They were more than happy to help her."

"What happened?"

"She showed up, out of the blue, confronted me in the diner one evening. I tried to deny it, but of course she knew me, even with a hairstyle and color change. I tried to explain, to apologize, everything to settle it, to let her be on her way, but she kept telling me about her lost ten years for something she hadn't done and how no one believed her. And she wanted a pound of flesh." Reed looked at the mayor. "Just like you. She was going to tell her story to the press back home, tell them who I was and what had become of me and what happened that night. And then my father's enemies would know. I couldn't let that happen.

"I picked her up at the motel, drove her to the church, told her we needed somewhere quiet to talk. We walked into the baptistry, and she started yelling at me, and I grabbed Walter's belt that was there—and, well, you know the rest. I wore gloves so there were no prints, but that damn earring..." She looked over at the mayor. "You should have left Hall alone. He didn't know anything about me. He was around me for booking and everything, and it was clear he didn't recognize me. But you wouldn't listen." Her eyes moistened and her voice suddenly cracked, and she yelled "*Why did she do that? I killed my best friend! Why did she make me do that*?" Carla Reed buried her face in her hands, her shoulders shaking.

Foster had been staring straight ahead. Now he turned to look at her. "You should have gone to prison instead of her," he said. "You ran and sold out your best friend. She was right to be angry with you, to hate you. And your dad should have made you face the consequences, not send you to another state and change your name. You were a spoiled brat. And you still are."

Carla Reed looked at Daniels. "I'm sorry, Chief. Really." She sniffled. Tears streaked her makeup.

"Me too." Daniels said. He nodded to the state troopers. They took the mayor and Carla Reed into custody, the click of handcuffs loud in the quiet of the moment.

CHAPTER THIRTY-EIGHT

CARRIE ANDERSON

FIVE HOURS AFTER THE MEETING AT THE church, Asa had been summoned from a quiet slumber by the jarring phone call. He'd arrived to find the police station quiet. Several officers were milling about with stunned, shocked looks in their eyes. It was never easy when it was one of your own.

Daniels was not immune. The chief wore his exhaustion like a mask to hide the anger and hurt. "She asked for you."

"Are you okay?"

"Sure."

"For what it's worth, I'm sorry."

Daniels nodded and sighed. "Yeah."

Carla Reed sat in a cell, her uniform replaced by a jumpsuit. She merely glanced up as Asa approached. "Rev."

"You wanted to see me?"

She nodded, and Asa motioned to the jailer to unlock the door. The young man did so but didn't bother looking in her direction. Asa walked in and sat on the cot beside her. "What can I do for you?"

"Guess my coworkers don't want to know me anymore," she said. "Guess I can't blame them."

"They're still in shock, I think," Asa said.

"What about you?"

"No, I'm not. *Disappointed* is the better word."

"The chief was right," she said. "You're a good detective. Tenacious and smart."

He nodded at the compliment. "What can I do for you, Carla?"

The former Carrie Anderson looked at the floor. "We had been out in the bar with friends. I got really loaded, worse than Tara, but you know how it is, you always think you can drive." Her voice was soft.

"You don't have to tell me this. You should have counsel present."

She didn't seem to hear him. She was back a decade before in a small Kentucky town. "He was suddenly there, and I couldn't react fast enough and he hit the bumper and twisted, rolled onto the windshield..." She put her hand to her face as though the memory was a physical pain.

"I panicked, Reverend. Tara had been knocked out, and I put her in the driver's seat and I ran. I told my father. He was so angry with me. He knew if it got out what I'd done, his enemies would bury me. And him.

"For two years he squashed it, kept it under the rug, a ghost that we feared would pop up with one wrong word. I told him I wanted to go turn myself in, especially when they were going to sentence poor Tara for something that I'd done."

"And your father refused?"

"Yes. He wouldn't hear of it. Tara got ten years and I wanted to call her, write her, talk to her. But I couldn't. I couldn't forgive myself. How could I expect her to forgive me? Then Daddy got sick and told me his plan. He was going to go to another state, hire a firm to give me a new name, a new identity. It cost him nearly everything, but he didn't care. He was dying by then, and he knew it. At first, I didn't think I could do it, but soon Carla Reed became me, someone who had the honor and bravery and smarts that Carrie had never had. And I thought it might put the ghosts of the past to rest."

"Then the mayor..."

"Yeah. He told me he knew, even showed me pictures of his father, one of the attorneys who had created Carla Reed. I thought it was over."

"But it wasn't."

She finally looked up. "He was a scumbag, Reverend. Making me...do things when his wife was out of town. But I had no choice. I couldn't let Carla Reed die. My daddy had put everything into her." Tears ran down her face. "I guess somehow I knew that one day it would catch up with me. I tried to postpone it. I hid the lab results when they came in and blamed the lab for being slow. Trying to avoid the inevitable, you see. Then I stood there and watched you lay it all out so neatly. And I knew." She looked at the walls of the cell. "The inevitable finally came."

"Yes, I suppose it has."

"Reverend, in the days to come, could you...pray for me?"

"Of course. Would you like to pray now?"

She shook her head. "No, not now. In days ahead, remember me. I don't know if God could ever forgive me."

"He can, if you ask and seek Him."

"What kind of person betrays a best friend?"

"A scared, drunk kid," Asa said.

"At least it's over," she said. "Perhaps it's best that it's out in the open now. In a way I'm free, I suppose."

"Perhaps."

"What about the mayor?"

"I don't know. He has his own set of problems."

She heaved a big sigh. "Thank you, Reverend Carter, for coming."

Asa rose. "Goodbye."

She gave him a quick smile, and the jailer opened the door. Asa glanced back to see her sitting on the bunk, staring at the floor before she disappeared behind him.

EPILOGUE

"THE COUNCIL WILL APPOINT AN INTERIM mayor until elections can be held," Kyle said, leaning back in his chair. "Some want you to do it."

"I'll pass."

"When did you suspect the mayor?"

"Well, they were both there at the motel, and, quite frankly, I didn't know for sure until the fingerprint came back."

"I don't understand why Chief Daniels didn't know about the fingerprint on the needle."

"Simple," Asa said. "Reed intercepted the lab results."

"Really?"

"Yeah. She didn't want them seeing anything in those reports. Neither did the mayor. So, they never made it to the chief's desk. I had to get Sgt. Mallory to get them again."

Kyle shook his head. "Hard to believe. They're probably going to take a plea deal."

"I figured so."

"Pretty amazing, you figuring all this out."

"When Violet told me she'd seen a second police car and then I connected the scar in the photo to Reed, everything began to fall into place. I just needed some proof. I didn't want the chief to have to deal with the idea of one of his own being the killer until I was sure."

"Then you brought in the state cops," Kyle said. "I heard the chief was getting the paperwork ready to send Carla to the Academy in a few months."

Asa nodded. "A shame."

"I came close a few times to asking her out," Kyle said. "Don't know if she would have accepted."

"Why not?"

"She wasn't a churchgoer, you know, and me being a minister and all."

"It wasn't meant to be, I guess. You'd have been dating a murderer."

The young minister seemed to think for a long moment. "Imagine her coming here and realizing that the mayor's father was responsible for her new identity."

"Had to be a shock when he sprang it on her. But then it was too late. My guess is, he kept his cards close until she was on the force, then sprang it on her."

"To think poor Walter almost got charged with murder."

"And I think she probably thought no one would be up there for a couple of days to discover the body," Asa said. "And she might have been right. Except you decided to take me on a tour."

Kyle brightened. "So it was me that kind of put a gnat in the pudding, as my grandma used to say."

"You could say that," Asa said.

"I hope God can forgive her," Kyle said.

"He can if she seeks it," Asa replied. "You should know that."

"I do. It's just that you always find yourself thinking that some people don't deserve it."

"None of us deserves it, Kyle. That's why John Newton called grace amazing."

Kyle got up. "Well, that one is solved. Until the next one."

"I think that's my last foray into detective work," Asa said.

"I hope not," Kyle countered. "It was a pleasure watching you work."

"I appreciated your help."

Kyle walked out of the office and was replaced by Mae. The secretary had a stack of papers in her hands.

"Now that the detective work is done, Pastor, there is the Lord's work to attend to. At least until the next body is found."

"I just told Kyle, that's my last murder case."

Mae sniffed. "Oh, pish-posh. Save it for someone who'll buy that." She set the papers down on his desk and walked out.

THE END

ABOUT THE AUTHOR

RICK NICHOLS IS THE AUTHOR OF SEVEN novels featuring former spy turned PI John Logan. In his spare time, he enjoys guitar, drawing, chess, golf, Go, and spending time with family. He is a veteran and lives in Florida.